"Chris, Chris, Chris," she said, and then fervently worked her lips and tongue and breasts and her entire body against me.

It was too much for a human male to bear. I got up, scooped her into my arms and headed for the bedroom. Her arms clung to my neck, frantically as though I might let her go. Little danger of that. It was obvious to both of us the way she was affecting me. She nibbled at my ear, and the heady perfume of her hair filled my nostrils. Where my fingers were touching her bare flesh, her skin seemed hot. The animal excitement that throbbed through her seemed to pass across to me, and I found myself trembling as I took her into the darkened bedroom and gently placed her on the bed.

7 DEADLY SINNERS

A Christopher Sly Mystery

Charles E. Fritch

WILDSIDE PRESS

Published by Wildside Press LLC
wildsidepress.com

Chapter One

I was sitting quietly in my apartment thinking about the dream job that had been tossed into my lap and really looking forward to it. I'd had interesting assignments before, but nothing like this.

Me, I'm Christopher Sly, private detective, six-feet-two-inches from bare tootsies to my sandy crewcut, with lots of muscle in between. Before I turned to detecting, I was an actor, an extra chiefly, doing stand-in work for the Tarzan movies, pulling oars as a galley slave, and so forth. But it was rough finding jobs, so I was also a stevedore, an oilfield worker, and a chauffeur for a nymphomaniac who had a jealous husband. It was the chauffeur job that decided me to get a position with a steadier income.

I thought of becoming a stud for underprivileged females, but I did the next best thing instead: I became a private detective. In a few instances, the difference was imperceptible, but for the most part the job was pretty dull and unromantic—until this latest job came along. From the brief description I'd had of it, it seemed I might be able to utilize my full talents

The doorbell rang. I figured it was Dave Keller the New York detective who'd offered me the job and pulled the strings necessary to get me in on it I was wrong.

I opened my apartment door, and there was a girl standing there. There was absolutely no doubt in my mind that she was a girl. Her body shouted GIRL from the top of her flaming red hair to the tips of her man cured toenails. I wasn't the least bit disappointed.

She flashed a friendly smile at me and said, "Are you Christopher Sly, the private detective?"

"I sure am," I said heartily. "Are you selling Girl Scout cookies? I'll take a gross."

The smile got broader and friendlier as she shoc her flame-tressed head. "No," she said, "but you're close."

Not as close as I'd like to be, I thought. She was wearing a tight black dress that looked like it was painted on, and my keen bachelor eyes couldn't detect a sign of bra or panties.

"My name's Naomi Burke, Mr. Sly," she said. "Make I come in?"

"Of course," I said, stepping back. "Come on i By all means."

The means she used was delightful to watch. She walked in, but it was more than a walk. It was poetry it was music, it was a way of life. She moved on high heeled shoes into the room; her woman's flesh fore and aft jiggling provocatively.

I closed the door and turned as she sat down on the couch and crossed her legs so that the skirt pulled up above the knees. She had nice legs, and nice everything else, too, that I could see. She was a solidly constructed girl. She followed the general pattern girls generally follow, but she was special and very generous in a couple of places.

"You're staring," she said, pleased.

"Yes," I admitted.

"They *are* good, aren't they?" She took a deep breath that threatened to rip the fabric of her dress. "I've had a lot of compliments on them. I suppose you're wondering why I came to see you?"

"The thought hadn't even crossed my mind," I told her. "It's been much too busy with other thoughts. The important thing is that you're here. Would you care for a drink?"

"I'd like that," she said. "Scotch on the rocks?"

"Scotch on the rocks," I said and went to the bar to get it.

I got out the booze, the glasses and the ice cubes but I wasn't really paying a great deal of attention to what I was doing. Naomi Burke had gotten up from the couch—exposing lots of white leg and thigh in the process—and was walking slowly about the room, peering at pictures and things. Once, when she bent over to inspect the record on the phonograph, the dress stretched across her nicely rounded bottom, and I almost dropped my glass.

Fortunately, Scotch on the Rocks is a drink that doesn't take much concentration to prepare, and I finally got two glasses ready and took them to to her. I was almost afraid to find out what it was she wanted. People who come to a private detective usually are in some sort of trouble, and maybe I'd find out this luscious creature was married and had five kids and the fact that she didn't wear panties meant that she merely didn't like to wear panties.

She took the drink from my hand, and her fingers brushed mine and lingered in what seemed a caress. It sent hot and cold goosepimples chasing up and down my spine.

"Thank you, Mr. Sly," she said.

"You're welcome, Miss Burke," I said. "It *is Miss* Burke, isn't it?"

"Yes," she said. "But you can call me Naomi."

I breathed a sigh of relief. That took care of a husband and five kids that could easily louse up a nice healthy seduction.

"And you can call me Chris," I said graciously, backing her up toward the couch.

She sat down, and the dress pulled up over her legs. She didn't bother pulling it down. I wondered if she were a real redhead. I sat down beside her, very close, our legs and thighs touching. I could feel the heat of her body through the thin dress, and my temperature started a skyward climb. She was a complex of feminine curves from top to bottom and back up again, and from my viewpoint the sight was breathtaking.

She sipped at her drink, and her lips came away from the glass, moist, sensuous, inviting.

"I'm one of the girls you're supposed to guard," she said.

I stared at her, not comprehending at first. Then the light dawned, and I said, "One of the starlets at Majestic Studios."

She nodded. "I thought we might — er — get acquainted," she said, "before some of the other girls get at you."

"It sounds like a great idea," I enthused. "Ever since you rang my doorbell I've been dying to know you better."

I'm a great believer in the direct approach. I took her glass gently from her hand and placed it with my glass on the coffeetable. Suddenly, I felt her hand on my leg, and I looked up to see her leaning toward me, her face tilted expectantly, her red lips slightly parted. Apparently, Naomi believed in the direct approach, too.

I put my arms around her, and she slithered into the embrace with quiet enthusiasm. I covered her lips with my own and held her close to me. Her body

9

molded against mine, and through the thin material of the dress I could practically feel the flesh underneath. But practically was rapidly not becoming what I had in mind. Her lips were working feverishly against mine, her body was squirming excitedly against me. She made soft moaning animal sounds. I forced her back onto the couch, and my hands moved across her, along the heaving breasts, the trembling hips, the expectant thighs.

"Chris, Chris, Chris," she said, and then fervently worked her lips and tongue and breasts and her entire body against me.

It was too much for a human male to bear. I got up, scooped her into my arms and headed for the bedroom. Her arms clung to my neck, frantically as though I might let her go. Little danger of that. It was obvious to both of us the way she was affecting me. She nibbled at my ear, and the heady perfume of her hair filled my nostrils. Where my fingers were touching her bare flesh, her skin seemed hot. The animal excitment that throbbed through her seemed to pass across to me, and I found myself trembling as I took her into the darkened bedroom and gently placed her on the bed.

She kicked off her shoes and quickly unzipped and wriggled out of her dress and threw that beside the bed. She held out her arms then and pulled me beside her.

10

"Chris," she murmured. "Oh, Chris, touch me, kiss me, do anything you want, anything but please don't stop."

I wasn't planning on stopping. In fact, I was just starting. And Naomi was helping.

With frantic desperation her fingers fumbled at my shirt, pulling it from my trousers, and then they moved to the belt. In seconds, there was no barrier between us, and our bodies drew together, her naked breasts flattening against my chest, her hips holding against mine.

Our mouths closed about each other, the tongues thrusting eagerly. I moved my hands along the length of her beautiful body, across the silky mounds of her female flesh where they lingered, and then moved on. I touched and stroked and caressed her, and she began to moan and tremble and shudder.

"Chris," she moaned. "Chris."

And we made love. Beautiful, violent love. Our bodies meshed, and her nails raked my back, and her teeth were like needles of fire burning into my shoulder. Her breathing became faster and rougher, matching mine, as her movement increased its delightful tempo, and she cried out in an animal excitement composed of sounds rather than words. I closed my eyes and buried my face in the pillow and held on, tossed by waves of emotion. She let out a moan that was low and deep and there was a sudden contraction of muscles and a sexual explosion, and then it was over and we were lying quietly together, limp and sweat-soaked, our hearts pounding, our breathing sighs of relief and happiness.

We lay unmoving for a few minutes, resting, eyes closed. Then, she murmured, "Chris, you were wonderful."

I pushed myself up on one elbow and smiled down at her. "You were pretty swell yourself," I said.

It was an understatement. I'd never before been with a woman filled with such wild animal excitement. She was breathing deeply, and small beads of perspiration stood on her heaving bosom. I bent to kiss her on the cheek, a passionate but gentle kiss that somehow seemed so anitclimactical that we both had to laugh. She pulled me back down to her and held me tight and purred like a contented kitten.

"I never want to let you go," she said in a happy whisper. "Never."

"That might be a little inconvenient," I said, smiling.

But I thought about Dave Keller, who was coming to visit me and tell me about my new job. I was glad he hadn't arrived so far, but sooner or later—and probably sooner, damn it!—he would be ringing my doorbell, and a job is a job. I recalled that Naomi had volunteered the information that she was one of the bodies I was supposed to guard. It would be nice being near Naomi and getting paid for it. It could turn into a beautiful friendship.

"We'd better get dressed," I suggested reluctantly. "I'm expecting company."

She pouted. "A girl?"

I laughed. "No, not a girl. By the way, how did you know I was assigned to guard you."

"Word gets around," she said, with a smirk that was supposed to suggest mystery. "Some of the girls were talking about it and wondering what you were like. They thought you might be a male Charlotte Rice." She made a wry face, and at my puzzled look, she explained. "Our chaperone, a little greyhaired lady who's very strict but who goes to bed early and sleeps like a log."

Her hand slipped along my leg. "But I can see you're different."

"Hey, that tickles!" I said, rolling over on the bed.

She got up. "May I use your shower?"

"Be my guest," I said gallantly. "In fact, I may even join you."

In fact, I'd be out of my mind if I didn't. She was standing nude beside the bed like some Greek Goddess just arisen from the sea, the tiny droplets of sweat beading her body and making it glisten even in the dim light of the bedroom.

"I wish you would," she said. "I get awfully lonely taking a shower by myself. Besides, you can scrub my

13

back, if you like."

"I like," I told her. "I haven't done a good deed all day."

"That's what *you* think," she grinned. "This way to the bathroom?"

"Uh-huh." I got up. "I'll get us some fresh towels."

I went to the linen cupboard to get some towels, and I heard the water running in the shower. When I got into the bathroom, Naomi was already in the shower stall and enough of her body showed through the obscure glass to make it seem very provocative.

I opened the shower door and said, "How is it?"

"Ooooh, wonderful," she cooed. The water came in many streams from the shower head and made rivulets along her shoulders, along her breasts and down her stomach. "Come on in."

I went in and closed the shower door behind me. It was slightly crowded in there, but I wasn't about to complain. Naomi had seized a bar of soap and was proceeding to make lather all over my body with it. All over, but she seemed to be specializing in certain areas.

"I like my men clean and healthy," she said. "And from the looks of things, you seem to be both." She moved her hands across my chest in a very distracting fashion, and then thrust the soap into my hand. "Your turn."

I took the soap and started soaping her shoulders

14

and her breasts and along her stomach.

"Mmmm," she murmured, eyes closed, "that feels so good."

"Yes," I said, a bit hoarsely.

When I was through with the front of her, she turned and I lathered her back and her firm womanly buttocks. And then suddenly, I found myself breathing more rapidly and losing interest in cleanliness.

"I have the feeling," Naomi said seriously, "that you are an emotional young man, Christopher Sly." She turned slowly. "I like that, but there are times when you should relax."

"It's hard when you're around," I told her.

She nodded, pleased. "I can tell. Maybe we should do something about that."

"Maybe we should," I agreed, but she was already in the process of doing something about it.

I leaned back in the shower stall, eyes closed, not listening to the sound of the water pelting us or the gurgle of the water going down the drain, aware only of the intense pleasure throbbing through my body. Naomi was in incredible girl, and very talented in many ways.

After awhile, she rose to her feet. "There," she said. "It's amazing how a warm shower will relax a person."

"Isn't it, though," I admitted, grinning at her.

I was about to grab her and kiss her in a brotherly fashion on the forehead, when the telephone began ringing. I grabbed a towel and walked swiftly out of the bathroom and into the living room, were the phone was.

"Is this you, Sly?" a male voice wanted to know.

I admitted it.

"This is Dave Keller. Sorry I'm late. I was delayed. Are you alone?"

"Yes," I lied.

I looked up to see Naomi standing in the doorway watching me, a towel held loosely and somewhat unnecessarily in front of her. No man could be alone with Naomi around; no man would want to be. She could just be in the room, doing nothing, and it would be very exciting. I turned my attention back to the phone.

"I'd like to come over now and talk to you about the job I mentioned earlier."

"Sure," I said. "Any time."

He hesitated. "There's a good deal more than I told you about it."

"I thought there might be," I said. "When will you be here?"

"A half hour okay?"

"Fine," I said. "See you in a half hour."

I hung up and looked to see Naomi pouting prettily. "Was that your girl friend?" she asked, in a heaven-help-you-if-it-is tone.

I laughed. "I don't have a girl friends. In fact, I

don't even like girls. The only reason you appeal to me is because you look like a boy!"

Nothing could have been further from the truth. She was holding the towel to her in such a way that it was practically useless as a covering, and the cloth had become wet and clinging and had pasted to her lush, rounded body.

"Lady," I said seriously, "if you keep looking at me like that, we're going to try for some sort of record tonight."

Her smile got wider, and she dropped the towel and held out her arms.

"Hey, I've got company coming. Business-type company. Even a private detective's got to eat," and at her grin, "Don't you have to get to bed early?"

It was incredible. Nothing I said seemed to have fewer than two meanings, so I decided to give up on the light approach. I went to her and took her shoulders in my hands and looked into her green eyes. Her skin was still warm and not entirely from the warm shower.

"I could stay in the bedroom," she said, "until your visitor left. I promise I won't listen."

"There'll be other times," I said. "At least, I hope there'll be other times."

She nodded. "Lots of them. You'll be living right in the same building with us, so there won't be any chance of escaping."

"Who wants to escape?" I said, drawing her close, feeling her warm, smooth flesh against me. Then, quickly, I pushed her away. "But you've really got to go."

"I know," she said, with a reluctant sigh. "They do keep pretty close tabs on us. I managed to sneak out, and now I'll sneak back in. Janet Hooper will cover for me; at least, she'd better, with what I've got on her!"

Women! I thought. I wondered if Janet Hooper was as good looking, and as uninhibited, as Naomi. Naomi was the only one of seven girls that I'd seen, but traditionally Hollywood starlets are well-shaped and exceptionally pretty. And I'd be among them, living with them, seeing that no harm came to them. I couldn't help but think that it was like giving a wolf the job of guarding seven young lambs from other wolves, but I had no intention of mentioning this analogy to anyone but my sleeping conscience.

I got dressed while Naomi busied herself in the bathroom. Then she came out and quickly slipped into her dress and sat down on the edge of the bed to put on her high heels. More than ever, it seemed as though she'd been poured into the tightfitting garment. The memory of her voluptuous nude body was still with me, and the tight dress seemed almost transparent to my remembering gaze.

She got up moved in close to me and put her arms

18

around my neck. I held her waist.

"We'll get together real soon, Chris," she said.

"Yes," I said.

"And Chris—" She hesitated. "Be careful."

I looked at her, puzzled. "About what?"

"I'm not sure, really. Maybe it's my imagination, but I have the feeling that there's something about this situation that isn't on the up and up. Your being hired to guard us, I mean. Maybe it's just my silly woman's intuition, but—"

I laughed and kissed her lightly on the nose. "I'll be careful," I promised. "Now, you'd better get along before you turn into a pumpkin."

It was a difficult metamorphosis to imagine, and I didn't bother trying. She pulled my unresisting head down to meet hers, and our lips collided, moistly, passionately, parted to allow greater intimacy. Even now, the feel of her body through the thin dress was very exciting.

We broke away and she walked to the door, hips moving the way female hips should move. She paused briefly and pursed her lips in a remote kiss, and then opened the door and went out. I could hear her high heels clicking along the concrete patio and past the pool.

Suddenly the apartment seemed very silent and lonely, and I went to make myself another drink, wondering what Naomi had meant about my being careful.

Probably just, as she'd said, her woman's intuition going astray—and yet there were some odd aspects of it that perhaps Dave Keller could clear up. Like what was his interest in it?, for example. And why the big deal of guarding a bunch of starlets?

I'd just poured the scotch over the icecubes when the doorbell rang. That would be either Naomi coming back for thirds, or Dave Keller to give me another kind of business, I decided. I was wrong on both counts. I threw open the door. A large, heavy-set man in a dark suit was standing blocking the doorway.

"I want to talk to you, Sly," he said in a low voice. It wasn't a request, it was a statement of fact.

He seemed pretty determined, so I said, "Sure, come on in."

Besides, there's one rule for survival I practice as often as I can, and this was one of those times: never argue with a man who's got a gun in his hand and is pointing the muzzle at your stomach!

Chapter Two

He was a big man, an inch or so over six feet, about my size, but the gun in his hand made him seem much larger. He made a motion with the gun, and I backed up into the living room. He came in and closed the door securely behind him.

He wouldn't win any beauty contests, but he wasn't something you might find in a zoo either. He had an ordinary, impassionate face, the kind you wouldn't notice in a crowd, topped by medium cut brown hair. From the way he walked he seemed wiry and agile, despite his size. He was watching me very carefully, as though I might try to take the gun away from him and toss him out on his ear.

He was wrong—at least just then. I may be a little stupid at times but, as the saying goes, I'm not crazy. I knew a little Judo and Karate, but I also know that the hand is not quicker than a speeding bullet.

"I don't suppose you're selling Girl Scout cookies either," I told him.

He grunted. "Very funny, Sly," he said, but I noticed

he wasn't laughing. "Who was that girl that was just in here?"

"What girl?"

I could see he was trying very hard to be patient. "The one who just left your apartment thirty seconds before I arrived."

"That was no girl," I said. "That was the landlady. Today is rent day."

"You're a real comedian," he said, thumbing the hammer back on his revolver. "In ten seconds, if you don't stop playing smart, you'll be a real dead comedian."

I'd been hoping to get him sore enough to take a swing at me with the gun. A guy can't shoot a swinging gun accurately, and it would get him off balance where I could pile up a couple of points for my side. It made me nervous to have people point guns at me. The weapon looked like a snub-nosed .38, similar to the one I sometimes carry, and I knew it could make a neat little hole where it went in, a great big hole where it came out, and a lot of damage in between.

"Because I'm a very patient man, Sly, I'll give you one more chance. Who was that girl?"

He was serious. Dead serious. I didn't know what the score was, but I had the urge to stay alive long enough to find out. I backed into a chair and tried to look casual.

"Her name is Naomi Burke," I told him. "She's a

starlet at Majestic Studios. Her phone number I don't have."

Warily, he sat himself in a nearby chair, holding the gun casually. "What else?"

"That's about it. Except she has a great figure."

"Why was she here to see you?"

I was honest with him. "I wondered that myself. She said she'd heard I'd been hired to guard a group of Majestic starlets, and she wanted to—er—see what sort of fellow I was."

The thought suddenly occured to me that maybe Naomi had a jealous boyfriend somewhere or even a husband she wasn't telling me about, and he'd hired this ape to do some damage to me. *Be careful,* Naomi had said, when she left. I didn't realize I'd have to be careful so soon.

"Okay," I said, "I've told you what I know about her. Now, I'd like to know a few things about you. Like what's the big idea of coming in here with a gun and asking me questions. What is it you're after?"

"You're hardly in any position to be asking questions," he pointed out. "Besides, you're not telling me the whole truth. She was in here a pretty long time."

"Look," I said exasperated. "I met Naomi for the first time tonight. I never saw her before tonight. She came in unexpectedly, we had a drink, we talked a little, then she left. She didn't tell me anything about herself. We just talked about—well, you know, smog, taxes, things in general."

"Did you go to bed with her?"

The question surprised me. "No," I lied.

He grinned his disbelief, then turned his attention elsewhere. "What about this job of yours? What is it, and why did they pick you in particular?"

"Majestic Studios has a group of seven starlets," I told him, "they're going to use to plug a picture called SEVEN DEADLY SINNERS. In two weeks they're all going out on the road to do some advertising for the picture. Meanwhile, the studio wants to see that they don't get into any trouble."

"Enter Christopher Sly," he volunteered.

"Right," I agreed. "Majestic, from what I've been told, considers these girls hot properties and can't afford a scandal. So they hired me as a watchdog. Why me in particular I couldn't say and still appear modest."

He considered this for a moment and then stood up. "Okay, Sly, I'll settle for that—for now, anyway. But I'll keep in touch with you. Meanwhile, keep your nose clean. Now, stand up."

I stood up. "What's your angle. Why are you so interested in Naomi Burke?"

"Turn around," he said.

"Look," I said, "at least you could tell me—"

He made a motion with the gun, so I shut up and turned around, facing the wall and wondering now what? Now what was not long in coming.

"I'll be seeing you, Sly," he said.

The last half of his sentence was forced out of him, so I knew what to expect. I started rolling with the blow just before it landed. But even so, the gun connected heavily with the base of my skull. My head exploded with a maze of fireworks and sound, and I reeled forward, reaching for the wall to steady myself. I felt myself sinking to the floor, and the darkness came...

The darkness was around what what seemed like a long time. And then Naomi Burke appeared in my mind. Naomi in the skintight dress, smiling seductively, holding out her arms to me. She was a dream, and I reached out for her, and suddenly the dream became a nightmare. She disappeared, replaced by jagged streaks of pain which flashed across my brain. I could feel the blood throbbing across my temples. My skull felt like it was coming apart at the seams.

"Feeling better?" a voice said.

A male voice, vaguely familiar. I tried to gather my senses. I was sitting, lying really, in a chair, and someone was placing cold cloths on my head and neck. I forced open my eyes and then closed them quickly again, wincing at the room lights.

"Take it easy," the voice said. "You got a nasty clout there. You'll be okay, though. Nothing serious."

That, I decided, was a matter of opinion. The man

with the gun had said he'd be seeing me. He was right. He'd be seeing me until I closed both his eyes for him and then pounded him through the pavement.

Experimentally, I opened one eye, then joined it with the other. I was still in my apartment. On the couch sat a thin man in a business suit, with greying closely-cropped hair and a mustache. He looked like he might be an insurance salesman.

"Dave Keller?" I asked him.

He nodded. "Too bad I didn't get here sooner. I missed the excitement, apparently. Anybody you know?"

"I never saw him before tonight. But I intend seeing him again—soon, I hope."

Dave considered this. Then he said, "Can I get you a drink?"

"Thanks. I could use one. You can also tell me what this is all about."

Dave went to the bar, fumbled around with bottles. "First, you tell me what happened tonight." He came back with drinks, handed me one, sat down on the couch with his.

I told him about Naomi dropping in to see me, and about the thug paying me a visit after she left. I went into more detail regarding my second visitor.

"Tell me, Chris," he said, when I'd finished, "did you and she go to bed?"

"You, too?" I said, beginning to get slightly annoyed.

He laughed. "It isn't just idle curiosity. Believe me, there's a definite reason for my asking."

"Yes," I said, "we did. But why?"

He got up, walked across the room and back before answering. "Let me ask you a question first. Did you ever hear of a man named Nick Matcha?"

I searched my memory. "Sounds familiar, but I don't remember where I've heard it."

"You probably read the name in the papers. Nick was deported to Sicily last year." He took a sip of his drink. "Incidentally, he was a member of the Mafia."

There was a moment of silence. "Incidentally?" I asked.

He shook his head. "No, not incidentally at all. You know, Chris, it's interesting how many people think the Mafia is a work of fiction, and those who do believe it think it was something out of the roaring twenties and isn't around any more." He sat down. "They're wrong, of course. The Mafia started out in 1915 as a patriotic group in Sicily, then degenerated into a gang of extortionists. They gave up writing extortion notes when dope peddling, bootlegging, smuggling and gambling became more profitable. No crime is too great for the Mafia—and even its own members are not immune to sudden, violent death, brutal beatings and torture."

I waited silently for him to continue.

"Nick Matcha was a member of the group. Nick had a girl friend. Nick was deported. The girl friend wasn't. Are you beginning to get the picture?"

"I think so," I said slowly.

"Nick was, of course, intimate with the girl. You might say they were—uh—very close. Even if Nick never told her anything directly, or talked in his sleep, it was inevitable that she would learn things about the organization. Things the government might like to know, things the Mafia wouldn't like the government to know."

"I see," I said.

' The girl disappeared," he went on. "She apparently realized her life was in danger, so she wisely ran as fast as she could. However, she's been traced to this area. More specifically, to Majestic Studios. And even more specifically than that, to one of those 'seven deadly sinners" you're supposed to guard."

I whistled at that one. "Don't you have a picture of her, or at least a description?"

He nodded and pulled an envelope from his pocket. "There's a picture of her in there, just the face and shoulders, and what statistics we know of her on the back. Nick wasn't too free with passing his girlfriends around."

"Then—"

"Then why don't we just contact her? Because we don't know which one of the seven she is. None of the girls matches the girl in the picture, whose name by the way is Carol Rutledge." He shook his head sadly. "People, especially women, can change their appearances so easily these days. She could change her hair color, her hairdo, use different makeup in different ways, maybe even have plastic surgery done on her."

"How about fingerprints?" I suggested.

"Fine," he said, "except we don't have any. She didn't have a record. In fact, there's only one identifying feature that's likely to go unchanged."

"What's that?"

He hesitated, somewhat embarrassed. "A diamond-shaped birthmark. She could have had it removed, but it's unlikely because of the —er—particular place where it is."

"Where is the birthmark?"

He told me, and I stared at him, wondering if I'd heard him correctly. "On her what?"

He nodded. "We got the information from a former boyfriend." He smiled. "Trying to find that will probably be the pleasantest part of your job."

"I'm looking forward to the search," I told him honestly. "I suspected from our phone conversation that I'd have to do more than just be a watchdog. The money you're paying me is very good."

"The job is very dangerous. It will undoubtedly have its pleasant moments, but remember the Mafia knows about it, too, and they're going to try and find her before you do. They'd have no compulsions about destroying all the girls, but they'd have to examine each one of them for the birthmark to make absolutely sure Carol Rutledge was among them—and that might be difficult in a wholesale slaughter. Besides, they'd prefer to do it quietly right now. Needless to say, the government would like to know about this girl, too."

"How do you fit into the picture, Dave?" I asked him.

He grinned at me and took out his wallet, flipped it open and handed it to me. "I'm not an FBI man, if that's what you thought. Just an ordinary private detective licensed by the state of New York. As far as I'm concerned personally, it's a job I'm doing for an insurance company. Carol Rutledge is carrying a hundred thousand dollars of life insurance, with the premium paid up for another month."

"And the beneficiary?"

"Nick Matcha, of course. You can see why the insurance company doesn't want anything to happen to Carol—at least for another thirty days, anyway."

I glanced briefly at his credentials, then handed his wallet back to him.

"I get it," I said. "A local detective could investigate without arousing suspicion, especially if everyone thought his job was something else — like being a watchdog for a bunch of movie starlets."

"Exactly," Dave Keller agreed. "By the way," he

continued testily, "you were chosen because of your —uh—shall we say your romantic reputation? It's all arranged for you to live in the house with them—it's a big thing, practically a mansion, that Majestic has rented, in the Hollywood Hills."

"Fine," I said enthusiastically, "when do I start?"

"Tomorrow morning. You report to Oscar Devlin at Majestic Studios around nine. Oscar is in on it, but as far as anybody else is concerned, you're there only to see the girls don't get in any trouble. Your methods will be your own, but I'll contact you from time to time for a progress report. You can get in touch with me through Oscar."

He glanced at his watch, stood up. "That's about it. How's the head?"

"What? Oh, I'd forgotten about it. Okay."

I went with him to the door. He paused. "By the way, about that birthmark — did you notice if Naomi?—"

I frowned, concentrating. "You know, I never noticed," I said finally.

"Well, you'll probably see her again. You can check it then." He made it sound so businesslike. "I needn't tell you the danger involved, Chris. The Mafia means business. If it suited their purpose, you could die in a hundred different ways, and sometimes not as swiftly as you'd like either; they've got experts, and they've had a lot of practice."

31

We shook hands and for the second time that night I promised to be careful. At first, I'd thought this was going to be a dream job, and there were some parts of it that fitted the description.

But with the Mafia around, it could also turn into a one-way nightmare!

Chapter Three

Majestic Studios was in the San Fernando Valley, at the end of a side road that lead into what was left of the wilderness. It was surrounded by a large wooden fence. I headed my Porsche toward the gate and stopped as a wooden-faced guard came out of his glass cage to inspect me, a clipboard in his hand.

"Christopher Sly," I told him. "Mr. Devlin's expecting me."

He checked a paper on the clipboard and nodded. "Mr. Devlin's office is in the big white building there," he told me, jabbing his finger toward a clump of buildings squatting nearby. "You can park out front. Mr. Devlin's secretary will take you in."

I thanked him and drove past the gate. There were several large American cars in the parking area, mostly Cadillacs and Lincoln Continentals it seemed. There was one Jaguar convertible, a red one. I snuggled the Porsche next to that, got out, walked to the buildings.

The white building was the largest, and it resembled an old Southern colonial mansion, complete with porch and pillars. A large sign said MAJESTIC STUDIOS in letters of gold. I opened the door and walked in. There was a deep colorful rug on the floor, uncomfortable-looking colonial furniture sprinkled strategically about, and portraits on the wall of serious-looking men and women in costumes of long ago.

Behind a large colonial desk set against one wall sat a very contemporary-looking blonde with horn-rimmed glasses, a dazzling smile, and a tight-well-packed sweater. Her legs were tucked under the desk where I couldn't see them, but I bet they were great.

"May I help you?" she asked sweetly.

"Mr. Devlin's expecting me," I told her. "My name's Christopher Sly."

"Oh yes, Mr. Sly," she said. "Just a minute, please, I'll see if Mr. Devlin is busy right now."

She punched an intercom button, waited for an answering "Yes?" and then said, "Mr. Christopher Sly is here Mr. Devlin." Devlin grunted something, and the girl said to me, "You may go in now."

"Thanks," I said, flashing her my most brilliant smile.

I maneuvered around the desk and went through the door into Oscar Devlin's office. It was a large room, with thick carpeting, more pictures on the walls, drapes framing French windows, one wall covered with book-lined shelves, an enormous polished mahogany desk, and several chairs scattered about. Behind the desk,

Oscar Devlin sat tilted back in a swivel chair, puffing a big black cigar and staring contemplatively out the windows at the studio lot. At my approach, he swiveled about in the chair, got to his feet, and extended a hand. His features split into a grin.

"Sly," he said, pumping my hand, "glad you could make it. Have a chair, boy."

He was young, probably no more than thirty-five, with long black hair slicked back and streaked slightly with almost theatrical touches of gray. He was wearing an expensive-looking blue suit, with an expensive-looking red tie fastened to the neck of an expensive-looking white shirt. He was short, probably not over five-five in his elevator shoes, and he looked like a small boy behind the huge mahogany desk. He peered owlishly at me behind oversize horn-rimmed glasses.

"Would you care for a drink?" he asked.

"If you'll join me," I said.

"Fine," he agreed, and stuck the cigar back in his mouth and jabbed an intercom button with an impatient finger. "Diane," he mumbled around the cigar, "Will you come in here, please."

"Certainly, Mr. Devlin," Diane said, and a moment later, she flounced in, and I discovered I was right about the legs. She had two of them, and both of them were sheer delights.

"A bourbon and water for me, Diane, and for Mr. Sly here—?"

"A scotch on the rocks," I said.

She was wearing one of those flouncy skirts that resembled a partly opened parachute, with acres of petticoats underneath. She walked over to the bar in one corner, and it was fascinating to watch the layers of clothing bouncing up down above those marvelous legs. A moment later she returned with the drinks, then left the room and closed the door behind her.

"Not bad, eh?" Devlin said.

"Not bad at all," I agreed, enthusiastically.

"My wife," he said.

"Oh," I said.

"Well, let's get down to business. Charlotte Rice is coming over in another twenty minutes. The studio car is picking her up. You've never met Charlotte, I imagine. She's the chaperone for the girls, and a very good woman, although a bit straight-laced. Probably just as well though, considering her job. It wouldn't do the studio any good to have any of the girls get into trouble."

I remembered Naomi mentioning Charlotte Rice, but I didn't want to tell Oscar that I'd already met Naomi.

"Does Miss Rice know why I'm here?" I asked him.

"No," he said. "Dave and I are the only ones."

And probably at least one other, I thought grimly, remembering the ape who'd slugged me.

"As far as the outside world is concerned—and the

girls themselves, for that matter," he went on, "you're a sort of guardian angel. You'll see to it that the girls don't get into any trouble, that no bad publicity results. But you'll also have the job of finding out which one of the girls is Carol Rutledge. I—uh—trust you'll be discreet in your search."

"With Charlotte Rice around, I'll have to be. Dave said I was to live in the same house with the girls."

"That's right. It's a nice little place, I'm sure you'll like it."

"I'm sure I will," I told him. "By the way, what's your angle, Oscar? I mean, why are you interested in finding Carol Rutledge?"

"Insurance," he said, "although not the same kind that Dave Keller is interested in. We've got a lot of money tied up in our picture, 'SEVEN DEADLY SINNERS' and a lot more in grooming the young ladies for possible stardom. The Mafia isn't something I want breathing down my neck; they could make a lot of trouble I can't afford. I want you to find that girl so I can get her and her problems out of my hair."

The intercom buzzed, and he jabbed a button.

"Miss Charlotte Rice is here," Diane said.

Oscar gulped his drink. "Better get rid of these," he said, placing his glass in a desk drawer. "As I said, Charlotte is a nice kid but a little bit stuffy. I'd hate to have you two get off to a wrong start."

I swigged mine, handed the empty to him, which he

placed in the desk drawer.

"Okay," he said into the intercom, "send her in."

The door opened, and Oscar and I stood up as Miss Charlotte Rice walked in. She had a firm, almost masculine walk, a determined setting of one foot in front of the other to reach a particular destination. She was almost a cliche of the old maid. She was wearing a plain, rather drab dress that managed to make a shapeless blob of her body from neck to well below calves. Her feet were encased in shoes designed for comfort rather than style. Her face was pale, without makeup, her blue eyes hidden under steel-rimmed glasses. Her hair was long and grey and pulled tightly along the side of her head to the back of her neck where it was fastened in a bun.

I had the impression that Miss Charlotte Rice wasn't really trying.

She paused for a moment in the center of the room. "Gentlemen," she said briskly. Then she went forward to pump Oscar Devlin's hand.

"Miss Rice," Oscar said, waving a hand in my direction, "this is Christopher Sly, the private detective who's going to watch over your girls."

She looked me over suspiciously, then seized my hand. The grip was firm and functional. "Happy to meet you, Mr. Sly," she said, staring at me. "To tell you the truth, however, I was expecting someone older."

"I'll get older, Miss Rice," I promised.

"Chris is a very good man," Oscar said.

Charlotte Rice backed herself into a chair and sat very stiffly there. "He may be a good man," she said, "but the fact is, he's a very young man. It would be wiser to get someone older, to avoid temptation."

"I'm sure I can control my emotions, Miss Rice," I told her.

She smiled tightly, without humor. "I wasn't thinking entirely of you, Mr. Sly. The girls are young, too, they're human—"

"Which is why," Oscar pointed out, "we need a good watchman for them. Chris is highly recommended for the job. I'm sure we can all put our trust in him."

There was such a tone of finality about his last statement, that Miss Rice merely shrugged. She stood up.

"Shall we go then? No doubt Mr. Sly would like to meet the girls and see his new home."

"I would indeed," I agreed.

I was thinking more about the girls than the house, and I hoped my enthusiasm didn't show in this direction. Oscar's secretary-wife had caused my blood temperature and pressure to rise, and I was rapidly getting in the mood to get to work.

After another few minutes of idle chit-chat, we said goodbye to Oscar and left. With a mighty effort, I managed to restrain myself from leering at the blond receptionist. Miss Rice probably wouldn't have approved. And neither would Oscar for that matter.

Miss Rice didn't have a car and had taken a cab to the studio, so we were to ride together to my new temporary home. She frowned in a disturbed manner at seeing the Porsche, but she didn't say anything, although she undoubtedly equated fast cars with fast people. She got in very sedately, taking great care that her skirt didn't rise to show any leg as she maneuvered into the bucket seat. We pulled out the the studio parking lot and headed for Hollywood.

It was mid-morning, and not many cars were out on the freeway. I had the top down, and we drove along without talking, the wind whistling about us. From time to time I glanced secretly at my formidable companion, trying to determine just how much trouble she was going to give me. I had to find a birthmark but I couldn't tell anyone it was really a birthmark I was looking for, and I felt certain Miss Charlotte Rice would not be in sympathy with my trying to search for what she would think I was searching for.

"Is something troubling you, Mr. Sly?" she asked suddenly.

"No, why?" I said, puzzled.

"You were staring at me," she said. "I don't like to be stared at. It makes me uncomfortable."

"Sorry," I said. "I was just thinking that I hope you and I will be friends."

"I don't see why we can't get along," she said. "You

and I are both concerned with one purpose—protecting our girls from any harm. That *is* your purpose, isn't it?"

"That's what they tell me," I said, straight-faced. "I'm here to do a job, and that's what I'll do."

We drove the rest of the way in silence, except for Charlotte Rice pointing out terse directions. The climbed into the Hollywood Hills, past expensive homes with lots of green space between them. At the top of one hill, with a magnificent view of the city, was our objective.

It was a white mansion set off the road with a large circular driveway curving among stately trees to the doorway. It was an impressive looking structure that probably cost Majestic a fortune to rent. I parked in the driveway out front, got out and went around to help Miss Rice from her seat. The skirt went up over her knees this time, but, gentleman that I was, I averted my eyes and pretended to not notice.

She took my arm, and together we walked up the steps to the massive oak door. She fished into her purse, found a key and applied it to the lock. I opened the door and followed her in.

There was a short hallway that was unpretentious, but beyond it was a room that could have been used as a railroad terminal. It was a large room, with thick carpeting on the floors, a huge chandelier hanging from the ceiling, doors on all sides, and a staircase that

41

started against one wall and spiraled upward to the second floor.

"The girls are probably out at the pool," Charlotte Rice said, leading the way.

We went through the farthest door, through a sort of alcove that led to the back of the house. I had the impression we were taking a shortcut and bypassing a maze of rooms. The last door opened onto the backyard, which had been fenced off by an eight foot concrete block fence. The house was old and stately and sort of dignified, but this setup was an addition that was intensely modern.

A large concrete patio confronted us, with exotic palm and banana trees strewn strategically about. In the center of the patio was a huge pool, built irregularly and surrounded by natural rocks and greenery to simulate a lagoon.

It was impressive, but even more impressive was the collection of young ladies scattered in and about the pool. Everyone of them was wearing the skimpiest of bikinis, and every figure in the group was magnificent. They looked up with interest as we approached them.

"Girls," Miss Charlotte Rice announced, and as they gathered I agreed wholeheartedly that they were without any question girls, "I'd like you to meet your new bodyguard, Mr. Christopher Sly."

I gulped and nodded greeting. I was speechless at the sight of all that female flesh so near and yet so far.

They were all girls, and yet they were individuals, too. Hairstyles and colors were different, body measurements differed, but basically the general pattern was the same. And there was one other difference, I reminded myself: one of them had a birthmark in an unusual place.

Charlotte Rice introduced them individually to me. There was Joanne Murray, a baby-faced blonde with a grown up figure; Christina Ekberg, a tall Swedish type, with long platinum hair; Mary Ellen Cuthbert, a southern brownette with a voice full of cornpone and chitlins; Carmen Cervantes with long jet-black hair and dark flashing eyes; Janet Hooper, with short light brown hair and a full tanned figure; Eva Slater, with a streak of white running through her coal-black tresses, and dark penetrating eyes; and Naomi Burke, a red-haired, smiling creature I'd met before.

The introductions left me breathless, with my heart pounding at the thought of living among these fantastic female creatures — and in anticipation of the great challenge that lay before me.

"Mr. Sly," Charlotte Rice said, and from the frown on her face I sensed she'd been trying to get through to me for some time. One of the girls giggled, and I blushed self-consciously. "Mr. Sly, I'll show you to your room now."

"Thanks," I said.

I glanced briefly at Naomi, who gave me a big wink,

then followed Miss Rice across the patio, forcing myself to not look back at the girls who had continued their sunning and splashing.

We went into the house, Charlotte leading the way, back through the alcove. We took a different turn this time, going into a large kitchen that had been brought up to date with all electronics had to offer. A pretty young lady with dark hair and flashing eyes and a pert nose was performing the chores necessary to making a meal.

"Annette," Miss Charlotte Rice said, "this is Mr. Sly. He'll be staying with us for a few weeks."

"How do you do, Monsieur," Annette said in a marvelous French accent.

"Happy to meet you, Anette," I said, which was perfectly true. Annette was a French doll.

"Annette is the only servant we have here," Charlotte told me as she led me away and the French girl returned to her chores. "She's an imported domestic."

"A what?"

"A girl who came to the U.S. agreeing to work as a domestic for a year. She's a very capable cook. I understand her father is a famous chef on the French Riviera."

"Hm," I said, noncommitally, but I was thinking of Annette the girl rather than Annette the cook.

Then I shook my head in consternation. I was going to have my hands full enough--in a manner of speaking—**without** adding to my burdens. It was the first time in my life I'd thought of a pretty girl as a burden.

We entered a corridor that had four doors running off it. Charlotte Rice opened one of the doors and went in, switching on a light.

"This is your room," she said. "The bath is next door. Annette and I have rooms across the hall. The girls' bedrooms are upstairs."

"Doesn't that make watching them a bit difficult?" I said.

"Not at all. You won't be in your room all the time. Besides, the stairway upstairs is old and creaky and it passes directly over our rooms."

"I see," I said, noting that this would also make *my* sneaking upstairs difficult.

"Did you bring all you'll need with you?"

"I have a suitcase in the car."

"Fine. If you need anything, I'll be right across the hall. Oh yes, lunch will be served in an hour in the dining room."

I wondered how thin the walls were, but I said only, "Thanks very much."

She went to the door, paused. "Mr. Sly—"

"As long as we're going to be neighbors, why not call me Chris," I suggested.

"Because I prefer to keep our association on a purely business level," she said. Her tone wasn't unfriendly, but it wasn't warm either.

"Oh," I said.

"Let me make myself clear, Mr. Sly," she said. "I am the chaperone here, and I'll not tolerate any—any goings-on. You're a young man—much too young for this particular job, but apparently Oscar thinks otherwise and he's the one who pays the bills—and with all these young girls around, undoubtedly you will be tempted to try and—I believe the word is 'make out.' I suggest you do your best to avoid this temptation, and I'm sure we'll get along."

"I think I get the message, Miss Rice," I said.

"See that you heed it," she said. "And while you're at it, stay away from Annette, too."

Then the door closed behind her, and I heard her footsteps go across the hall and the sound of her door opening and closing. Apparently, Miss Charlotte Rice had a severe case of spinsterhood and probably virginity, neither of which were likely to be cured, at her age and with her attitude toward the good things in life. There were eight lovely girls living under the same roof with me and—chaperone or no chaperone—I was going to see them, and not merely because it was my job, either.

I took from my breast pocket the photograph Dave Keller had given me. Carol Rutledge—a pretty, smiling girl about 25 years old, with light brown hair and eyes that were mischievous and sparkling. She looked like a girl I'd like to know. Nick Matcha had good taste.

But I didn't recognize the girl in the photograph as any of the 'seven deadly sinners' I'd seen out by the pool. As Dave had pointed out, it's easy for a girl to change her appearance—a different haircolor, different hair styling; even a different arching of the eyebrows would change her, and with what Carol had at stake plastic surgery wouldn't be too much to expect.

Except there was the existence of a small diamond-shaped birthmark. When I found that, I'd have the girl I was looking for.

There was a soft knock at my door. Hastily, I returned the photograph to my pocket, before answering.

"Chris—" Naomi said.

I put a finger of warning to my lips. She slipped inside, and I closed the door behind her.

"Old lady Rice probably has her ear to the wall right now," I whispered.

Words weren't necessary for what we had to talk about. Naomi threw her arms around my neck and pressed herself close to me. She was wearing a skimpy white bikini that showed off everything but a birthmark, and the feel of her very female body against me was pleasant and stimulating. Our lips met, worked against each other, and I could feel the fires start.

She broke away. "I'm in the first room at the head of the stairs," she whispered huskily. "Can you come up tonight, when Rice is asleep?"

47

I nodded. "A herd of wild chaperones won't stop me." I didn't mention a herd of creaky stairs.

"By the way, do you know a fellow—" and I described the ape who cloppered me in my apartment, after asking about her.

She thought a moment. "No, I don't think so. Should I?"

"Not necessarily," I admitted.

"Well, I've got to change for lunch. Miss Rice informed us that with a man in the house, we'd all have to be decent young ladies. No more eating in bikinis or walking around in underwear." She blew me a kiss from the doorway. "Later," she said.

I frowned at a sudden thought. "Charlotte Rice said I was your *new* bodyguard. That means there was one before me. What happened to him?"

"Oh, didn't they tell you," Naomi Burke said brightly. "He was murdered!"

Chapter Four

I brought my suitcase in from the car, unpacked, and put things away, including the picture of Carol Rutledge which I placed face down under a pile of underwear. The bedroom was good-sized and comfortably furnished. It had a single bed, a writing desk and lamp, a few chairs, some landscapes on the walls, a dresser, a walk-in closet, and no windows. In one corner was a small portable television set on a stand. It was a functional room and not very exciting without a lovely female to dress it up.

Apparently, these were the servants' quarters, and in a sense I was a servant, along with Charlotte Rice the chaperone and Annette the cook.

While I was arranging things, I heard the squeak of the stairs as bodies ascended and descended, and I decided that Charlotte was right: it would be difficult for any of the girls to sneak out at night without me hearing them. And—unfortunately—for me to sneak upstairs at night without Charlotte hearing me!

It would be easier if Charlotte were on my side, and

I considered telling her why I was really here. Except the idea would undoubtedly shock her to the core, if she had one.

"You see, Miss Rice," I pictured myself saying to her, "I'm not really a lecherous coot. I just want each one of your girls to take off her clothes and—"

I shook my head. It was impossible to imagine me saying anythink like that to her, and even more impossible to imagine her being sympathetic. It would be dangerous trying—dangerous to Carol Rutledge, who might even run away, change her features again so we could never find her.

Having one of the girls on my side would be a definite advantage, though. Possibly Naomi. She seemed eager to please. But I'd have to check her for the birthmark first. Tonight, if I could get past those creaky stairs.

Meanwhile, I had to learn to find my way around the house. With fifteen minutes to go before lunch, I started out on the expedition.

The first turn led me into the kitchen, where Annette was busily preparing an army-sized meal for nine hungry people. She was standing on a small stool reaching into a high cupboard, and she presented a very intriguing picture from the rear. She was dressed in a black uniform trimmed in white, and as she reached, the skirt pulled up on the gracefully curved legs encased in sheer black stockings. She had a full round bottom that shifted provocatively with each delicious movement.

"Can I help you with that?" I asked her.

"Oh!" she said, startled.

The stool tottered precariously, and I rushed to catch her as she fell. She turned as she fell and I caught her about the waist and let her slide down against me until her feet were touching the floor.

She was a very solidly constructed young lady, and I found myself reluctant to let go. Her head was tilted up at just the right angle, and I had a desire to kiss those full red lips.

"Monsieur startled me," she said.

I decided to let her go, which I did. "Sorry," I said. "I was just wandering around, and I came in here accidentally. Do you mean you feed all these people by yourself."

Annette waved her arm in a casual gesture. "It is not so bad. My father taught me how to cook for people. He used to be a chef in Paris. And with all these wonderful electrical appliances I have to do very little work really. I put the food in the oven, and the oven cooks the food until it is done. Afterward, the garbage disposal unit takes care of the garbage, and the electric dishwasher takes care of the dirty dishes. All I have to do is serve the food."

I sat down in a nearby chair and watched her continue those feminine movements. "How long have you

51

been here, Annette?"

"Just two weeks, monsieur. This is my first job in the United States."

"You speak English very well."

"But of course. I studied it in school. I always dreamed of coming to America, and I wanted to be ready." She grinned shyly. "I—I thought maybe I could get in the movies."

"Maybe you can. You're very pretty."

She hesitated. "Can—can monsieur help me get into movies?"

I did a little hesitating myself, and during that time I tried not to look at that voluptuous figure working under the uniform.

I was honest with her. "I probably can't do very much, but I do know a few people in the industry, and I'll be happy to put in a good word for you."

With a grateful cry, she unexpectedly threw herself at me, arms around my neck, and the chair went over backward with a loud crash. Black-sheened legs, white thighs and a black garter belt flashed across my vision as we struggled to entangle ourselves. We were just getting to our feet, when I looked up to see Miss Charlotte Rice standing in the doorway looking very stern and very unhappy at the scene she was witnessing.

"Annette," she said icily, "I think you'd better get on with lunch—and it would be most prudent of you to avoid any future wrestling matches with Mr. Sly."

"Look, it was an accident," I said.

"Lunch will be ready in a few minutes, Mr. Sly," she said. "Shall we go in?"

I sighed. "Sure," I said.

I cast a deploring look at Annette and followed Miss Rice through the corridor.

"I told you to stay away from Annette," she said, when we were alone. "She's in this country for a probationary period, and if she does anything morally wrong during that time she can be deported."

"It was very innocent," I insisted. "An accident."

"I hope you're not accident prone, Mr. Sly," Miss Rice said.

It reminded me. "What happened to the former guardian of the girls?"

"He was killed," she said, matter-of-factly. "It had nothing to do with his job here, of course. Apparently, the man had enemies. He was found one morning lying face down in the pool, dead."

"Did the police find who did it?"

"Not yet," she said.

"Are you sure it had nothing to do with his job here?"

She looked at me. "What would it have to do with watching over seven young girls?"

I couldn't answer that one without telling her about my assignment. "I don't know," I said, "I was just wondering. By the way, where is the phone?"

"There are three phones. One upstairs in the hallway, one in the library, one in the kitchen. I'd suggest you use the one in the library."

Since Annette was in the kitchen and the girls were upstairs, I thought that might be her suggestion. "Are they all connected together?"

"There are buttons that will connect one line with another. But don't worry, I never listen in on other people's conversations."

I was going to open my mouth and lie that that wasn't what I'd had in mind at all, then thought better of it. Her tone was matter-of-fact, not indignant.

We went into the living room where the girls were waiting for us. They had all taken off their bikinis, and had put on clothing that covered them more, slacks or skirts. They were chattering busily among themselves, but when we walked in, the chattering stopped. Apparently I was still somewhat of a curiosity to them, for seven pairs of lovely eyes swiveled to watch my progress as I went to one end of the table, sat down, I forced a bright smile at the assembled beauties, aware that Miss Charlotte Rice had seated herself opposite me and was watching carefully.

I recalled that the girls were severely restricted as far as dates were concerned, until after the picture opened. They would attend the premiere and then be let loose upon the masculine world. Till then, I was the only male in the area, and my job—among other things—was to chase other males away. It gave me a feeling of power; the girls' lack of male companionship would help me find Carol Rutledge.

We ate lunch, we chatted idly, the girls talked among themselves, occasionally Miss Rice would grunt some answer to a question, and Annette bustled about with soup and salad and so forth.

I took the opportunity to watch the female faces around me, trying to figure which one might be the girl I was looking for. To my right was Joanne Murray, the baby-faced blonde whom someone had apparently told looked like another blonde named Marilyn, because her gestures and mannerisms were a la Monroe. Would this be the type that Nick Matcha would pick for a girl friend?

Except, I reminded myself, if Carol Rutledge changed her features, she would also change her habits, even put on an act.

Or develop a Southern accent, I added silently, as demure Mary Ellen Cuthbert smiled sweetly and asked me if I would pass her the "buttah."

Or possibly it could be Christina Ekberg, the tall Swede. She was taller than some of the others, and built like an amazon. I wished I knew what Carol's figure looked like; it would help.

Then there was Carmen Cervantes with the long black hair, who kept glancing at me with eyes that threatened to devour me alive.

And Janet Hooper with the brown hair and the slim tanned figure, who sat aloofly and only glanced at me occasionally. I wondered if I made her nervous, if maybe she suspected what I was really there for, if perhaps she might be the girl I was looking for. She was a pretty girl, and what was it Naomi had said to me about her?—"Janet Hooper will cover for me; at least, she'd better, with what I've got on her!" Blackmail, and for what reason. It was possible that Naomi knew that Janet was the girl friend of a Mafia member, or perhaps it was only that she had had plastic surgery done, or—

I glanced at Janet Hooper with possibly more than passing interest, and she met my eyes briefly and then turned away. I'd have to ask Naomi about that. It look promising.

Across the table from her was Eva Slater, with the band of snow white running through her otherwise black hair. Eva was a girl who would stand out in any crowd. Surely, Carol Rutledge would want to blend into the crowd and not go to theatrical extremes to be noticed—unless, of course, this was the sort of reasoning she'd planned on.

The simple fact was, I'd just have to look for the diamond-shaped birthmark. There were only seven places to look, but getting the view might prove difficult.

Naomi would be first on the list. As I thought of

her, I looked at her, and she seemed to be smiling in a subtle, mysterious fashion. It would certainly simplify matters if she were Carol Rutledge, but I wasn't sure I wanted the job to be that easy. Every one of these girls was a doll in her own special way.

The lunch continued to its conclusion, with only one outstanding incident. Joanne Murray was wearing a blouse that wasn't cut particularly low, but the neckline was wide, and when she bent to retrieve a fallen napkin, the blouse parted obligingly to show a pair of creamy breasts unrestrained by a bra. I wondered if she'd done that for my benefit, or whether it was accidental, and whether the rest of her would be as easy to see. In any event, my curiosity was aroused, and I was more determined than ever to look into the matter.

Chairs scraped back, and we adjourned. Naomi looked at me, then hesitated, glanced at Charlotte Rice and went out to the patio. The girls drifted off, singly and in pairs. Joanne Murray turned to me.

"Care for a ping pong game, Mr. Sly?" she invited.

That wasn't the game I had in mind, but it was a start. "Okay, but first I've got a phone call to make—if I can find the library."

"Through that door," she said, pointing, "and on the other side of the living room. I'll get into something more comfortable and see you in the patio."

I wondered what her more comfortable clothing

57

would consist of. It was a pleasant thought. It was also very pleasant watching her walk away. I wondered if she didn't believe in panties as well as bras.

I went in the direction indicated, found myself in the large room I'd compared to a railroad terminal, and walked through a pair of double doors into the library. I closed the door securely behind me.

Two of the walls were covered with books. One had a fireplace built of heavy-built stone. Another had French doors, with drapes drawn across them. There was a grand piano in one corner, and a huge desk near one wall. The telephone was on the desk, a white plastic phone with a row of buttons.

I picked up the receiver, and one of the buttons lit. I dialed a number, waited.

"Majestic Studios," a pleasant female voice said.

"Oscar Devlin's office, please," I told her.

There was a click, and a buzz, and another female voice came on, also sweely but with a definite trace of sensuality, "Mr. Devlin's office." I recognized her as Oscar's secretary-wife who had impressed me so much when I visited the studio.

"This is Christopher Sly," I told her. "Is Oscar in?"

"Yes, Mr. Sly. Will you hold on, please."

Oscar Devlin came on like gangbusters. "Hello, there, Sly, how's it going. You out at the house."

"Yeah," I told him. "I thought I'd report that I've become one of the family here and that everything is

58

under control."

"Have you—er—done any of the research we talked about?"

"Not yet, but it looks promising. By the way, you didn't tell me the last bodyguard was murdered."

"Didn't think it was important. Probably somebody had a grudge against him. Pumped a few .38 slugs into him and pushed him into the pool."

I recalled that the ape who'd paid me a visit in my apartment had carried a .38 special. Oscar could afford a casual attitude. If I wound up face down in a pool, he'd only have to hire a replacement.

"Do you suppose—" I started to wonder aloud if it could have been the Mafia's long black hand pulling the trigger. But then I remembered that there were two other phones connected in with the line I was using, one in the kitchen and one upstairs. I also became aware that there was on the line someplace the subtle sounds of someone breathing. Or else it was my active imagination.

"Well," I said casually, "that's about it. I'll give you a call if anything interesting happens."

We said goodbye, and I waited until he hung up, the phone still at my ear. There was the more pronounced sound of breathing, and then a click as someone who had been listening in hung up.

I replaced the receiver in its cradle and stood there for a moment wondering which one of the girls had been listening in, and why. Another thought was rapidly occuring to me, that maybe Carol Rutledge would be so desperate to avoid being found out that she would resort to murder to escape detection.

Like the murder of my predecessor, for example.

And me, for another!

Chapter Five

I made my way back into the kitchen, where Annette was busy putting dirty dishes in a washer. She looked up and smiled pleasantly.

"Anything I can do for monsieur?" she asked.

I stared at those lovely French features. She had an innocent child's face, with large liquid blue eyes mascarad to make them look more provocative. I stared also at the full French body straining at her maid's uniform, and somehow I refrained from asking her what was really on my mind.

"Annette, did anyone come in here to use the phone a moment ago."

She shook her head. "No, monsieur. I have been here, and no one came in."

That still left the upstairs phone and a couple of other possibilities: Annette could have been listening in out of curiosity; it could have been Charlotte Rice, who had heard me say I was going to make a phone call and she was busy playing a defensive mother hen.

Or, yet, it could have been Carol Rutledge.

"Oh, there you are," a voice said behind me, and I looked around to see Joanne Murray's blond head peering through the doorway. She glared at Annette, then returned her attention to me, coming into the room and grabbing my arm possessively. "How about that ping pong game?"

I gulped. Joanne's something-more-comfortable was a bikini halter that was almost useless as either a restraint or a covering, and a pair of the tightest white short-shorts I'd ever seen.

"Yeah," I managed. "How about that?"

She took my arm and led me through the alcove and out into the patio. The afternoon sun was shining warmly, and a gentle breeze rustled green banana palms. There were three girls sunning themselves at the edge of the pool. Tall, willowy Christina had returned to her white bikini and was stretched out on a deck chair, her long blonde hair streaming in a golden cascade over the edge of the chair. Carmen was sitting beside the pool, stretching, luxuriating as the golden rays of the sun caressed her magnificent dark-skinned body and lost themselves in the darkness of her coal black hair. The third girl was Janet Hooper, who had looked at me strangely during lunchtime. Janet's short brown hair was fluffed with wild abandon to frame a pretty, sensitive face, and her slim figure bore two slim pieces of cloth in strategic places. As we passed her, she glanced up briefly and for a moment I thought

I could detect a wild animal quality shining through those normally sedate eyes.

I had decided that, gentleman that I was, I would let Joanne come close to winning a game of ping pong. However, she had two factors on her side: she was an expert player and I found myself fighting to keep up with her; and she was wearing a costume that made it difficult for me to concentrate on the game.

With every movement, her breasts jiggled up and down and/or sideways, and when she bent over to pick up the ball, the view was fantastic. The halter was secured by straps running under her arms and snapped in back, and as we played the straps slipped lower and lower, and every once in a while we would stop the game so she could pull them up again. It was at one point where I had delivered a particularly fast ball in self-defense and she was reaching to swing at it with all her might, that the halter unsnapped and fell to the ground.

The ping pong ball hit her paddle with a resounding whap, as she returned it expertly and ignored the fact that her breasts were bare. The score was 20-20 and so was my vision, but somehow I managed to hit the ball back over the net to her. They were firm, full breasts and they danced in unison as she hit the ball back to me, as I gave it back to her, as she hit it back to me—

"Joanne!" came a stern voice from the opposite

end of the patio.

Startled, I looked up and the pingpong ball hit me low in the stomach. Miss Charlotte Rice, looking very stern and self-righteous, was marching down the concrete patio toward us. I noticed that Joanne had retrieved her dropped halter and was busy putting it back on. I thought this might not be a good time to offer to help.

"Joanne," Miss Rice said, "your conduct is disgraceful. Playing ping pong naked to the waist. The idea is disgusting."

That was a matter of opinion, obviously, but I said, "It was an accident. We were playing a game here, and the law of gravity just — "

"And as for you, Mr. Sly," she said, turning on me, "you seem to be having more accidents today than is good for you. One more like that and I'll see to it that Oscar replaces you with someone else."

With that, she marched off down the patio and disappeared.

"The old biddy," Joanne said, reaching around her to fasten the snaps holding the halter in place. "She's just jealous because she hasn't got anything to show off."

That could be, but the job was just getting interesting, and I hated to get pulled off of it just then. Besides, I needed the money. The longer I put off looking for the birthmark, the more dangerous it was for

Carol Rutledge. With time running out the Mafia might just decide to take a chance and kill all of the girls.

Joanne came up to me and thrust her breasts into my chest giving me something more pleasant to think about. "Will you help me with this. I'm having trouble fastening the snaps."

I reached around her under her arms and fumbled with the snaps. The fact that she was pressing herself against me and moving her body didn't help a bit. Finally, I got them together, and started to step back, but her arms went around my neck and she pulled herself to tiptoe to kiss me warmly on the lips.

It was an unexpected surprise, and I looked up to see if Charlotte Rice had been watching. Charlotte didn't seem to be around, but I noticed Janet Hooper glaring in my direction.

"Thanks," Joanne said.

Gently, I unwound her arms from me. "You're welcome," I said, a little hoarsely.

She smiled. "You like me, don't you?"

I nodded.

"I'm glad. Most men like me. I've got sex appeal. Some people say I could be another Marilyn Monroe. I affect men the way a meatball affects a dog. It's just natural, I guess."

"The most natural thing in the world," I agreed. "In fact, I was going to suggest that maybe we might talk about it later—you know, just the two of us."

"That would be nice," she said thoughtfully. "Most men I've met seem to think I'm just a sex boat, without any brains. I'm sure Miss Rice wouldn't object if I don't wear a bra in my own room."

"I don't see how she could," I agreed, "especially if we don't tell her."

I looked up to see Janet Hooper looking at me in that strange way I couldn't seem to analyze. Then she turned away, got up and walked toward the house, my eyes following her lithe movements.

"Do you know Janet very well?" I asked Joanne.

She shook her head. "Not very well. When I first got here, she seemed pretty friendly, but then I guess she got angry with me for asking her so many questions."

That was interesting. "What questions did you ask her?"

She shrugged. "Oh, just questions. You know, about where she came from and who her friends were."

"I see."

"Some people even think I look like Marilyn Monroe," she said. "What do you think?"

"Better than that," I said. "I think Marilyn Monroe looks like you."

She smiled, pleased, and then frowned. "What?"

"I'll explain later," I told her. "Right now, I've got to get to work."

I walked across the concrete patio, where the other two girls were. Christina had stretched her long legs out and was lying with her arms under her head, her eyes closed, her amazonian body soaking up the sun's rays. Carmen was watching me with those dark eyes of hers, and she gave me a brilliant smile as I looked at her.

I went into the house and into the kitchen, where Annette was puttering about. I wondered what she would look like in a bikini.

"Annette, what room is Miss Hooper in?" I asked.

"The second on the right, monsieur," she said, looking wonderingly at me.

"Thanks," I said.

I went into the living room and crossed to the stairs. I hesitated, then started up slowly. Boards creaked underfoot, and I knew that the sounds were magnified in the rooms underneath. In the daytime, Charlotte Rice wouldn't know whether it was one of the girls or me, so I walked boldly up the stairs to the top and down the corridor to the second door on the right.

I knocked softly and waited. The sounds of footsteps approached, and the door swung open. Janet Hooper stood in the doorway, wearing a bathrobe over her slim body and a puzzled and surprised expression on her face.

"May I come in?" I said.

"What is it you want?" she said coldly.

"I want to talk to you," I said.

"What about?"

I forced a laugh. "About smog and taxes, if you like. May I come in?"

She hesitated, obviously curious. "All right," she said.

I walked in, and she closed the door. The room was similar to my own, but larger and furnished more luxuriously. I sat down on the bed and looked at her, standing uncertainly at the door.

"What is it you want?" she said.

"I just thought we might have a talk," I said. "You don't seem to like me."

She moved away from the door, went to the dresser, lit a cigarette, took time to puff on it. "I'm sorry if it hurts your vanity," she said.

"And yet when I was out on the patio just a few minutes ago," I continued, "you looked at me—how can I describe it?—hungrily."

She laughed and came to sit down on the bed beside me. The bathrobe fell apart to reveal slim, tanned legs. Involuntarily, my eyes fell upon the legs, caressed them. She noticed my interest, but she made no move to pull the bathrobe together.

"Tell me, Mr. Sly," she said, "do I appeal to you—sexually, I mean?"

The question startled me, but I said, "Yes, of course," and as long as we were going in for the direct

68

approach, I put my hand on her leg.

I could feel her skin tremble beneath my touch.

"Looking for something?" she said calmly.

"As a matter of fact," I said, moving my hand, "Yes."

"Let me help you," she offered, and she unfastened the cord of her bathrobe and threw open the folds of cloth to reveal her nude body underneath.

Her breasts were small, but firm and well-shaped. Her stomach was flat. Her hips were graceful curves.

"Tell me, Mr. Sly, does it give you a thrill?"

I stared at her.

She threw the folds of bathrobe around her, and stood up, wrapped the cord securely around her waist.

"You men disgust me," she said, "with your incredible vanity. You thought I was looking at *you* downstairs. You're wrong. I was looking at your friend, Joanne, and hating you because she likes you instead of me. I almost had her once, and maybe I could have had her again if it weren't for you. Do I make myself clear?"

I stood up. "I got the message, Janet," I said sadly. "You're trying to tell me you like to play with girls instead of boys, is that it?"

"That's it," she said. "Now, will you get the hell out of here and leave me alone!"

I paused at the doorway.

"I'm sorry," I said.

She didn't answer. I went out into the hallway and closed the door behind me. It was a shame, a damn shame. She was a pretty girl, and I hated to think of that slim figure going to waste.

But at least it did eliminate one of seven suspects. Only six more to go.

I went back down the stairs and into my room, closed the door and sat down on the bed to think. Naomi was still high on the list of targets. Then there was Joanne, who had expressed interest in a get together. And four others I hadn't yet laid the groundwork for. It promised to be a busy week.

For a moment I stared at the suitcase protruding from beneath the bed. It didn't stick out very much, just enough to remind me that I'd put it completely under the bed where it wouldn't be visible. Someone else had moved the suitcase, and possibly other things, in a search through the room while I was away.

I wondered who and I wondered why, and then I got up in a sudden panic and went to the dresser drawer and looked under the pile of underwear.

The picture of Carol Rutledge was missing!

Chapter Six

That afternoon Lieutenant Prine of homicide paid me a visit. It was not a social call. Prine never paid social calls on Private detectives, and especially on certain private detectives.

"I'd like to talk to you, Sly," he said, adding: "alone."

"Sure," I said. "Let's go into the library."

We went into the library and closed the door behind us. For a moment, Prine wandered around, looking at the pictures and the books. He picked up a gold cigarette box from the grand piano and examined it, then set it down gingerly.

"Nice place," he said.

"Yes," I said.

"How'd you manage to con yourself into a sweet setup like this?"

His attitude annoyed me, as it always had, but I tried to be patient.

"I was picked," I said. "For my talents."

He grunted in amusement. Then he sighed and sat

down in an overstuffed chair. "It's not fair," he said. "I work and slave on the force for years pounding a beat before I even become a detective. Then more years before a promotion—"

"Shall I put on some violin music?" I said.

"—and you get the gravy," he went on, ignoring me.

"Life is cruel," I admitted. "Did you come all the way up here to tell me the sad story of your life?"

"No, I came all the way up here to see what you know about the murder of Frank Sheldon."

"Frank Sheldon?"

"The private detective who had this job before you arrived," Prine explained. "He was here about ten days, and then they found him in the swimming pool with four .38 bullets in him."

"I don't know anything about him," I said. "Only that he was killed. Sorry I can't help you."

"I thought that possibly, since you carry a .38, you might have killed him so you could take over his job here."

"Very funny, Prine," I said. "You'd like to pin a rap on me, wouldn't you?"

"I'd love to," he said. "Unfortunately, I don't think you did this, but if I find one that you did—"

"Well, you won't," I said, trying not to show my exasperation.

He shrugged. "We'll see. Meanwhile, what about Frank Sheldon?"

"What about him? I've told you all I know."

Prine rose from his chair and walked across the room. He was a small man with a large manner. His blond, greying hair was neatly parted over one eye and combed back with precision. He turned.

"Sheldon made a lot of enemies in his work. A lot of people would have liked him out of the way, perhaps even to the extent of killing him to accomplish that. But there's another angle."

"What's that?"

"His job here, the same job you now have. What is there about this job that could have killed him?"

I forced a laugh. "Lieutenant, this is a simple bodyguard job, except for the fact that the bodies number seven and they're all very lovely."

He shook his head, unsatisfied. "No. The situation smells like a fish market. You're up to something, Sly, and I want to know what it is."

"You've got an active imagination, lieutenant, but you're wrong." I thought of adding: "as usual" but I managed to restrain the impulse.

"You know," Prine said slowly, "sometimes I wonder if we're both playing ball on the same side, or if we're playing the same game. You seem to have the glamorous notion that you're a big shot private investigator who can take the law into his own hands. May I remind you that I'm a policeman hired by the citizens to protect them, and your persistent lack of cooperation only makes my job more difficult."

"You certainly may," I said, "and I want you to know that us taxpayers really appreciate the fine job you're doing."

He glared at me silently for a moment. "Okay, Sly," he said slowly. "One of these days you're going to be in trouble, and I'm going to be there to put in the thumbscrews. Remember that."

"I'll think of it constantly," I said.

He turned, paused at the door. "I don't believe you're telling me the whole truth," he said, "but we'll leave it for the time being. I wonder, though, if you've considered that if Frank Sheldon was murdered because he had this job, that you may be in line for the same treatment."

"Wishful thinking, lieutenant. There's no big mystery here. The only .38s the girls carry around here are on their chests."

He grunted. "I'll see you later."

"Anytime, lieutenant," I said. "Always happy to see you."

Annette showed him out, and I thought about what he'd said. I'd already considered the possibility of it. Sheldon could have come close, or even have discovered who Carol Rutledge was. The Mafia could have done him in, or even Carol herself to prevent the detective from telling anyone. In fact, it was more than possible: it was likely.

Worse, there was a disconcerting but somewhat inevitable conclusion to be reached. If *I* got close— and I certainly expected to—the murderer would undoubtedly try to do the same thing to me!

"Monsieur?"

I looked up from my thoughts to see Annette standing in the open doorway, looking very pretty and uncomplicated.

"Dinner, monsieur," she said.

"Be right there," I said.

One of the girls at the table would be Carol Rutledge. If I'd had any doubts that she was among the "seven deadly sinners," the doubts had been dispelled by the disappearance of her photograph. Apparently, she had listened in on my phone conversation with Oscar Devlin and had become suspicious enough to search my room while I was with Janet Hooper. It showed, at least, that I was hot on the trail.

One thing was certain: the girl I was after was not Janet. She'd proved that very graphically by showing me a place on her trim body that didn't have a birthmark. The memory of that slim, youthful figure was still fresh in my mind, and it was a shame that it would go to waste. Her skin was smooth and her curves, while not spectacular, were sleek, and outwardly she seemed to hold the promise of many pleasures. It was mismating of design and function, like a sportscar being used as a garbage truck.

I wondered if there was something in the photograph that was a legitimate clue to what Carol Rutledge looked like. Perhaps a subtle tilt of the corners of the mouth during a smile, or a crinkling around the eyes, or maybe something unnoticed because it was too obvious. Or more likely, she'd stolen the photograph merely to be on the safe side.

Dinner passed as had lunch, with idle and aimless chatter. Mary Ellen Cuthbert sat next to me this time, and busied herself asking me questions regarding my profession as a private detective. She was a demure Southern girl with an accent that almost required subtitles, but she had medium length brown hair and a pretty face and had on a red and white crinkly dress with a tight bodice. I made up a few exciting stories for her, mainly to avoid looking at Janet Hooper, who was busy making a point of avoiding me. I caught Naomi's gaze at one point, and I could sense she knew something was up.

Annette had apparently inherited a wealth of culinary knowledge, for the meal was delicious. She was a very talented girl, and I wondered how far her talents extended. I watched her move about the room and decided she'd look very nice without her clothing. I might even look into that—if I had time, which was beginning to seem rather unlikely.

The phone rang, and Annette went off to answer it. She returned, saying it was for "Monsieur Sly," so I excused myself and went into the library to answer it.

"Hello, Chris," a masculine voice said, "this is Dave. How are things?"

"Not bad," I said. "I've been trying to generate some good will. So far I've eliminated one out of seven, though."

"Not bad, for the first day. I assume you checked it thoroughly."

"Thoroughly enough," I said.

He laughed. "Need any vitamins?"

"I may," I said. "It would help if there were some other pictures." I didn't want to tell him the one he'd given me had been stolen. "How are things from your end?"

"About the same. The insurance company's anxious. Oscar is anxious; time is running out and he expects the world to end. By the way, Oscar said you phoned him earlier today."

"I got a little anxious myself. I understand the former bodyguard was killed."

"I told you the job was dangerous," he said. "The—er—organization I mentioned isn't going to let a simple murder stand in its way."

"If it was the organization," I said. "Another theory occurred to me, that maybe the other bodyguard was getting close and one of the girls did it."

There was a sharp intake of breath that wasn't Dave Keller's. I didn't waste time on preliminaries. I just dropped the phone and ran out of the library. The kitchen or upstairs? I wondered. I chose upstairs. None of the girls were in sight. Apparently, they had adjourned. I took the stairs two and three at a time and rounded the curve where the phone was. It was on the hook.

Disappointment flooded me. Either I'd made the wrong choice, or whoever it was had decided to hang up and beat it. I took the phone off the hook.

"Chris, hello, Chris, are you there?" Dave Keller was saying.

"Yeah, Dave, sorry," I said. "Someone was listening in from another part of the house."

"Did you discover who?"

"No, but I will." I noticed that a nearby door was ajar slightly, and I wondered if there was someone behind that door listening, someone who perhaps had been listening in and had heard me coming and ducked into the room.

"Yell, if you need help," he said.

"Right. I'll get in touch with you if anything new develops."

I hung up and stood silently for a moment in the hallway. On the other side of that slightly ajar door someone was moving, making only the slightest of noises. With swift, silent strides I crossed the hallway and threw open the door.

It was a room very similar to Janet Hooper's. And

standing in the middle of it, with only the bottom part of her bikini on, was a very surprised and puzzled Eva Slater.

We both stood there for a moment, looking at each other. Eva's long black hair hung down her back, with the dead white streak traveling all the way from forehead to where the hair ended. She had a solid body, with large breasts standing out proudly, unrestrained. Her waist was narrow, flaring to spectacular hips, tapering thighs, smooth curves of legs. There was no baby fat left on Eva Slater. She was all solid, functional, well-designed woman.

Her dark eyes regarded me quizzically, but she made no move to cover her nakedness.

"I was about to go for a swim," she said finally, "unless you have some other suggestion."

I closed the door behind me. If it was Eva Slater, or even if it wasn't, this seemed like it might be a good time to find out.

"I have another suggestion," I said, moving toward her.

"Then I suggest you lock the door, so we won't be interrupted," she said calmly.

She was right. An interruption would not be welcome. I locked the door, turned back to her. She was smiling at me, but it was a smile of defiance.

"One thing, however," she said. "I'm used to having *men* make love to me, men who know what they want and take it no matter what. If you're an amateur, you can just leave now and we'll forget it."

"I've had experience," I told her.

Her voice was mocking. "Have you? Prove it, then."

I stepped toward her to prove it. Her attitude was beginning to annoy me, but her body was getting more desirable by the second. It was so close, so smooth and rounded and full. I reached out for her.

She drew back her hand and struck me across the face, laughed and then moved away. I didn't expect the blow, and I got the full force of it, and my cheek stung. I stared at her, not fully understanding.

She wasn't angry. She struck a provocative pose and moved ever so slightly so that her breasts jiggled with the movement.

"Surely you're not giving up?" she said. "You discourage very easily, Mr. Sly."

"Who said I was giving up?" I said determinedly.

I reached her in two strides, grabbed both wrists in my hands. She struggled to pull away, but she made no outcry, and she was still smiling defiantly at me and those deep eyes were busy probing mine.

"What experience have you had?" she said tauntingly. "With drunken high school girls in the back seat of cars? You can't make out when you find yourself with a real woman, can you?"

She wrenched one of her hands free, and made a

swipe at my face with her nails. I ducked and automatically swung a fist to block her attack. The fist struck her on the shoulder, and she reeled onto the edge of the bed.

She held her shoulder with one hand, sitting on the bed, her legs stretched out before her. There was no sensation of pain reflected in her face.

"Now," she said in satisfaction, "you're beginning to show some spirit."

I stared at her, the truth beginning to grow on me. There was a theory that all women secretly want to be raped. With Eva, it was neither a theory nor a secret. She'd invited me in, even locked the door to make certain we wouldn't be disturbed. But she wouldn't give me anything. It would have to be taken forcibly, or not at all.

I hesitated.

"Well?" she said impatiently.

I wondered if Nick Matcha would go in for this sort of thing, and I stared at her half-nude tempting body resting on the edge of the bed, the breasts and the stomach rising and falling with breaths of anticipation coursing through her. Rape and the infliction of pain was nothing new to the Mafia, and with Eva Slater around, a member could get in lots of practice.

And whether I liked the method or not, I had to find out if she was Carol Rutledge!

She got up from the bed and turned away. "Forget

it," she said. "You're not a man, you're a—"

I sighed. It was something that had to be done. Savagely, I reached out and gave her a resounding slap across her bikini'd bottom. She turned in sudden surprise, and I grabbed her arm roughly and whirled her all the way to face me. I entwined the thin material of the bikini in my fingers and yanked it savagely from her body.

"Chris—" she said, wonderingly.

I didn't listen. There was a job to do, and I wanted to get it over with as soon as I could. Forcefully, I pushed her down on the bed, and then forced the breath from her with the weight of my own body. She gasped with pleasure at the roughness of me.

I played my part well, although my heart wasn't really in it, and when it was over I was exhausted from the effort.

She propped herself up on one elbow, shook her black and white hair where it had fallen across her forehead, and looked at me.

"Not too bad, for an amateur. You show promise."

"Thanks a lot," I said drily.

"We might even try it again," she suggested.

"We might," I said, but I knew we wouldn't.

Eva was not Carol Rutledge. I'd made certain to check that fact. That left five others, and I hoped the four I hadn't come in contact with didn't have any outstanding peculiarities that would make my investigation as difficult as in the cases of Janet Hooper and Eva Slater.

"You'd better leave," she said.

She was putting her bikini on once again. Cautiously, I unlocked the door and peered into the hallway. I took a last look at Eva, then slipped out into the hall.

"I wondered what happened to you," a female voice said.

I froze, thinking for an instant it might be Charlotte Rice, with either a shotgun or my walking papers. It was Naomi, coming up the stairs, frowning, her lovely body encased in a sunsuit.

"I was just having a chat with Eva," I said weakly.

"I'll just bet you were," she said, unsmiling. "Which was it this time, chains or whips?"

"Naomi—" I said, reaching for her.

"Don't touch me," she said, evading my grasp. "I thought we could have ourselves a relationship, but if you're going in for this sort of stuff—"

She went into her room and closed the door in my face. I heard the lock click shut. Apparently, she meant it. I wanted to say something, but I just stood there dumbly staring at the closed door, knowing there was nothing I could say. I couldn't explain to her why I'd been in the bedroom with Eva Slater, because I still didn't know for certain that Naomi was not the girl I was looking for. There was only one sure way to find out about that, and under the circumstances this was going to be more difficult than I'd thought.

It would be a matter of wooing her back, of winning her confidence—and at the same time seducing four other girls and trying to keep from getting killed by Carol Rutledge and/or the Mafia!

Chapter Seven

That night in my dreams a bedroom door opened and closed, and I was in a room with four beautiful young girls. There was Joanne Murray, the baby-faced blonde with the soft, rounded curves that demanded to be fondled. Next to her was Carmen Cervantes of the olive skin, her dark eyes flashing promises of animal ecstacy. Beside her was Christina Ekberg, her platinum blonde hair and white skin glowing in the dim bed-doom lighting. Mary Ellen Cuthbert followed, demure but willing. And Naomi Burke, pouting, holding back from the rest and yet wanting to come to me, wanting to love and be loved.

They were all naked and together they glided toward me, breasts rising and falling, hips moving in a provocative rhythm, intent on one purpose. Five pairs of female hands reached out for me, and I knew that my search would soon be over, that one of these girls would be the one with the diamond-shaped birthmark. All I had to do was discover which one. I reached out for the closest one—there was a sound—and the girls disappeared!

I opened my eyes and stared into the blackness of my bedroom. It took a moment to reorient myself, to realize that the girls had appeared only in a dream, and that a sound had awakened me. I lay very still on the bed, listening.

There was silence and darkness, and after a few seconds I decided it was only my imagination. Then I heard the sound of a bare foot brushing the floor only a few feet away, and I became instantly alert.

It could be Naomi, coming to make up—or Carol Rutledge coming to kill me before I exposed her.

My gun was in the drawer of the dresser, and I'd have to stretch to reach the lamplight on the table at the other side of the bed. One advantage was that whoever it was couldn't see me any more than I could see her. Stealthily, I swung the covers from me and sat up on the bed, silently wincing as the bedsprings squeaked.

The footsteps paused, and I could hear breathing a few feet away.

"Monsieur?" a female voice inquired softly.

"What?" I blurted.

"Sh!" the voice insisted. "Monsieur, it is Annette."

"Annette, what in the world—" I began. And then: "Wait, I'll put on a light."

"Oh no, Monsieur," she said hastily, and I felt her bump into me, grip my arm and sit down beside me on the bed. "No light, please."

The accent was unmistakably French, and she was unmistakably girl. She was apparently wearing a negligee, a very thin one it seemed from the feel of her warm skin pressing against my leg.

"If Miss Rice discovered me in here, she would have me sent back. I like it in this country. I want to stay."

"Then why are you here?" I said softly.

I felt her hand touch my pajama'd leg, and I almost jumped.

"Because I like you, monsieur, and I am lonely. Do you mind?"

Gently, her hand moved along my leg.

"No," I said, "I don't mind at all. In fact—"

I reached out and took her shoulders in my hands and pulled her closer to me. The nightgown was a wispy thin diaphanous, and I would have loved to see her in it. But it was also a pleasure to feel her in it.

"Oh, Monsieur," she murmered as our lips met.

We kissed gently, with partially open lips. Our tongues probed and danced. Her arms went around me, pulling me closer to her, and my own hands wandered along the expanse of nightgown, feeling the warmth of the skin it barely covered. I ran my hands along her forehead and her chin and neck and her hair, picturing it as I'd last seen her with those lovely liquid and expressive eyes looking at me.

Her hands were busy too, and I could feel myself starting to tremble as she fumbled with the buttons of my pajamas.

I pushed the thin material from her shoulders and let my searching hand slide under the nightgown. Her body quivered and she twisted her shoulders so that the nightgown fell away completely and she was nude from the waist up.

I moved against her, reveling in the warm softness of her woman's flesh pressing against me. The nightgown parted some more, and impatiently I removed it from her and let it fall to the floor.

I touched her smooth skin, my fingers flowing along her body, exploring the curve that sloped down to her waist and across her stomach, and she began breathing raggedly and sighing and making movements of anticipation.

Her lips found mine again, and we kissed hard and violent. I relaxed on the bed, and she followed me down until we were lying side by side and then suddenly no longer side by side.

The world became beautiful without shame, passionate without violence. Our bodies moved with the rhythms of love, starting at the base of a crescendo and then building higher and higher, increasing in tempo until it seemed we were riding the very crest of passion ...

And then suddenly it was over, and we parted and lay side by side once more, relaxed, the room silent except for our breathing.

She moved away from me suddenly and sat up on the bed.

"I must go," she said, and began pulling on her nightgown.

I touched her naked arm with my hand. "But—"

"No, please." She bent over me, and her searching lips found mine and pressed them briefly. I could hear her standing up, cording the thin gown around her. "Tomorrow," she whispered, "do not act as though anything has happened between us. Miss Rice is a very suspicious woman, and I would not want her to suspect."

"I'll pretend you don't even exist," I said. "Will I see you again?"

"You will see me again," she promised.

She moved across the room.

"Annette?" I said, on impulse.

She paused by the door. "Yes, Monsieur?" she whispered.

I hesitated. "You're very nice," I said.

"Monsieur is very nice, too," she said softly.

The door opened silently and she went into the hallway. I saw her nightgown-clad figure silhouetted briefly against the dimly-lit corridor, and then the door shut and darkness and silence returned.

I lay in the darkness, thinking of how wonderful it had been to be with a young girl who didn't have a mess of psychological problems to contend with. It was especially nice after being with Janet and Eva and the frustrating episodes with those two.

I almost asked Annette if she knew if any of the girls had a birthmark, but at the last minute I decided it not only ungentlemanly under the circumstance, but unlikely that the French girl would know. I might ask her tomorrow, though, if I could do it secretly. It wouldn't be something I'd want Charlotte Rice to overhear. I could understand Annette's not wanting her employer to know about the secret tryst she and I had.

I felt very relaxed and not mad at anybody. I just lay there, letting sleep drift over me as my eyelids became heavier and heavier and the sounds of the world became less distinct. I wondered if I could get back to that dream I'd started in which four beautiful young girls were coming at me with fire in their eyes. Not that I needed them just then, but it was still a pleasant thought.

I half-heard the door open, but I wasn't sure whether it was only in my dream, or whether Annette was coming back for seconds. It wasn't until a flashlight glared into my eyes that I realized it was neither.

Chapter Eight

I closed my eyes against the brilliance of the flashlight, and fought to struggle awake.

"Chris," a familiar voice said.

I reached out and pushed the flashlight down toward the bed, and I could see Naomi Burke standing beside the bed, dressed in a skirt and blouse.

"What in the world are you doing here?" I wanted to know.

She sat on the bed beside me. In the dim light her face looked troubled. I hope she hadn't seen Annette sneaking out of my room.

"I couldn't sleep," she said. "I was worried about you."

"About me?"

She nodded. "And about the fight we had. Maybe it was silly of me, but I was jealous. I didn't want any other woman to have you, and I was angry because you were in there. Besides, Eva's desires are a little bit different from most other girls."

"I discovered that," I said.

"I knew you weren't the type—at least you didn't seem to be. So I began wondering why you did it."

"And?"

"And I decided you must have a reason that wasn't sexual."

She paused expectantly, and I said: "Did you decide what the reason was?"

"No. Maybe you wanted to get information. Remember that woman's intuition when I first met you, when I thought you might run into trouble? I have that same feeling now." She ran her free hand along my chest, idly. "I'd do anything I can to help you, Chris."

She looked very serious and sincere bending over me like that. I reached out and pulled her head down to mine and kissed her gently on the lips, and then she placed her head on my chest.

"You know," she said, "I can't really feel alone with you here, not in the same house with the other girls and with Old Lady Rice snooping around every corner. Could we take a drive someplace in your car. Just a short one, and maybe park and take a look at the lights of the city?"

It sounded like a wonderful idea, a chance to really relax and let the world go spinning on its dizzy way toward the dawn of a new chaotic day. I glanced at my watch: one-thirty. Besides, maybe I could put my trust in Naomi, and the search for the diamond birthmark would come to a close.

The thought surprised me. I was trying to get myself out of a job in which I'd have to be intimate with lovely girls — and why? Because I liked to have Naomi's head on my chest, that's why, and because I was getting old and mellow and sentimental, and maybe even falling in love.

"Okay," I said, "but only for a couple of hours."

She stood up. "Rice is a heavy sleeper, but you'd better not turn on the lights, just in case. I'll hold the flashlight while you get dressed."

"But point it in some other direction. I'm not an exhibitionist."

She laughed lightly and pointed it at a nearby wall. I got out of bed, stripped off my pajamas, and dressed quickly. I put my .38 special snugly in its belt holster and buttoned my jacket over it.

I nodded to her and we went to the door and she snapped off the flashlight. We stood close together by the door, listening. It was nice having her so close to me, and on impulse I held her and kissed her again. I'd decided I was going to tell her. I would ask her if she had a diamond-shaped birthmark, and she would undoubtedly say no and offer to show me. I'd look, of course, because Dave Keller wouldn't be so sentimental and he'd want to know if I'd checked it.

A disturbing thought occured to me: suppose, just suppose, Naomi was really Carol Rutledge and she did have a birthmark. It meant she was also the one who had been listening in on the phone, and maybe had even had something to do with the former bodyguard's death.

Annoyed with myself, I shoved that last thought from my mind.

"I don't hear anything," she said.

I slowly turned the doorknob and edged the door open a crack. The hallway was dimly lighted and showed no one in sight. I opened the door farther and glanced up the other way. Charlotte Rice's and Annette's doors were both closed, and no light showed from underneath.

I stepped out into the corridor and signaled Naomi to follow me. Gently, I closed the door again. The house was quiet, and the soft whisper of our feet on the carpeting seemed loud to my ears.

We used the flashlight to cross the expanse of living room, into the front hallway, then eased the large door open. The night was clear and cool, the sky black with brilliant silver pinpoints of stars. There was no traffic on the road. We went out to where I'd parked the Porsche, got in. I started the car, put it in gear, and moved off onto the road.

"There's a turnoff down here a ways," Naomi said. "I'll show you where. There's a sort of plateau where we can park."

The lights of the Porsche stabbed twin shafts into

the darkness, sweeping across the silent road and the sentinal trees guarding it. I glanced in my rearview mirror and saw a car's headlamps rounding a curve we'd just taken. A half-mile from the house, I swung onto a side road, and a few seconds later the other car accelerated past on the main road, and roared downhill.

A cluster of trees gave way to an open spot with a panoramic view of the city. I pulled of the road, doused the lights and the motor. Silence drifted over us. The lights of the city stretched out below us like a glowing necklace.

I put my arm around her, and she placed her head on my chest and gazed out the window. "It's so peaceful up here. It's as though we were apart from the rest of the world, just the two of us."

I nodded and felt very content with the softness of her besides me, the delicate feminine smells of her. Up here it seemed as though the troubles of the world were remote, that there was really no such thing as the Mafia or murder, and violence was a madman's dream.

For awhile we watched the winking lights of the city and the carlights tracing patterns on the night air, and then she said, "You want to know something, Chris. I think I'm falling in love with you."

"Funny," I said, "I've been thinking the same about you."

She turned her head up to me, and I took it in my

hand and kissed her tenderly.

"I know you've got a job to do," she said, "and I'll try not to interfere. But really, if there's anything I can do to help—"

I made a sudden decision. "There is. Will you do something for me, without asking any questions, something that may seem strange?"

"Of course," she said, "but—"

I took the flashlight in my hand, pointed it down at her legs, and switched on the light. "Will you pull up your skirt, please?"

She stared at me, puzzled, and then laughed. "I don't mind, of course," she said incredulously, "But in a *sportscar?*"

I was beginning to feel uncomfortable, but I'd started it, so I was determined to go through with it. "The skirt, please?"

"Well, okay," she said.

She reached down, grasped the hem of her skirt and lifted it slowly, tantalizingly up along her legs. Her legs were bare and very smooth and lovely, and the unveiling process was delightful to watch. I moved the flashlight back, so that the rays spread out to reveal the full sweep of her limbs.

The skirt rose up above her knees and then past her thighs. She was wearing thin white panties, and the rays of the flashlight penetrated it as though it didn't exist.

"Now what?" she wondered aloud.

My voice was hoarse. Even after my recent escapades, the sight of her bare flesh so close and so available was beginning to affect me.

"Remove the panties please," I said.

"Christopher Sly," she said, a little bit annoyed by the mystery, "this isn't a highschool peepshow. You've got something more than sex on your mind. Now what is it?"

I sighed defeat. "A diamond-shaped birthmark," I said, and at her quizzical look: "One of the seven girls has a diamond-shaped birthmark on her—that is, in the area of—I mean—"

"I can imagine where," she said, dryly. "And how many girls have you checked so far?"

"Just Janet Hooper and Eva Slater. Neither one of them is the girl I'm looking for."

"And you think I might be the one?"

I shrugged. "It's possible."

"I don't have birthmarks, there or anyplace else, Chris."

"I'd like to take a look, anyway, if you don't mind."

"That would remove the challenge," she said, lowering her skirt. "No, I think I'll make you work for it, Chris. No free peeks tonight. But tomorrow—"

"Naomi, this is no laughing matter. A man was killed, perhaps because of it, and maybe Carol Rutledge will be killed too if we don't get to her in time

97

—if *you're* not Carol Rutledge."

"Who?"

"Carol Rutledge, the girl I'm looking for."

"I'm not."

"It's easy to prove it."

"All right," she said, finally, "although this takes a lot of the romance out of it."

She lifted her skirt again to reveal those magnificent legs of hers, hooked her fingers in the panties and pulled down on them, working them over her hips, down her thighs and legs and then stepping out of them.

"Go ahead," she said.

"I'm going , I'm going," I said

I swung the flashlight to look, and I looked. In the close quarters of a Porsche this is not an easy task, but I managed it with Naomi helpfully shifting to a more accessible angle.

There wasn't a birthmark in sight.

"Anything else you'd like while you're in the neighborhood?" she asked, drily.

Reddening, I switched off the flashlight and sat up in the seat. "I'm sorry, Naomi, but I had to make sure."

She touched my arm. "It's all right, Chris. I was just teasing you. You can look anytime you want. Except I hope you won't be content with merely looking."

"You can depend on that," I promised. "Meanwhile, there's the problem of Carol Rutledge. It's not you, and it's not Janet Hooper or Eva Slater, so it must be one of the remaining four."

She sighed. "And I suppose you'll have to seduce every one of them."

"If I have to," I admitted, more glumly than the situation demanded.

She laughed at that. "You sound as though the prospect doesn't please you."

"I'm sure the prospect pleased Frank Sheldon, too," I reminded. "Look what happened to him."

"You think his death had something to do with the case you're on?"

"I think so, and I may be the next target. That's one reason I've got to find this girl as soon as I can."

"Do you have any idea which one it could be?"

"Not the slightest. All I know is, when I find the birthmark I find Carol Rutledge."

"I've been thinking, Chris," she said. "Wouldn't it be easier if we told Charlotte Rice about it. Maybe she could just have a—well, a sort of inspection like they do in the army?"

"I thought about that," I admitted. "Trouble is, I have a hunch that just mentioning it would send Charlotte Rice into a panic. And even if it didn't do that, it might send Carol Rutledge rushing off to the nearest airport, but fast."

She nodded. "I suppose you're right. I guess you'll just have to do it the hard way."

I grinned at that and kissed her lightly on the forehead. "Thanks for your vote of confidence."

"To think," she said, "I was jealous, when all the time you were just doing a job."

"Well, I *am* human, too, you know."

"I know," she smiled, putting her head on my shoulder. "I've noticed."

I placed my arm around her and held her close. The night was dark and very silent. Below us, the lights flickered quietly.

"Kiss me, Chris," she whispered.

I kissed her. It was a warm, gentle kiss, beginning with nothing more than a fond brushing of lips. Then she turned within the circle of my arms and her hand dropped onto my leg. Her tongue probed my lips seeking entrance, finding it. Her breasts were hard and firm against my chest.

I remembered the sight of her bare legs in the flashlight beam, soft, warm, feminine legs that were now pressing against me intimately. I thought of those marvelous breasts so close to me and automatically I reached to touch them.

Eyes closed, she sighed and without taking her lips from me, she took my hand and guided it into her blouse, under the loosefitting bra. My hands moved, caressing her, and I could feel desire welling up within me swift, certain and demanding. I placed a hand on her leg, under her skirt, feeling the warm flesh respond to my touch. I moved my fingers along her skin—

There was a sound from outside the car, a sound that might have been a footstep.

I froze, listening, and then I tried to pull away from her.

"No," she said, clutching me, "don't stop. Not now!"

"I'm afraid he'll have to, miss," a male voice said.

We broke apart, and I turned toward the voice, reaching for the gun at my belt.

"Hold it!" the voice said.

I held it. I didn't have much choice. The snub-nosed barrel of a .38 revolver was pointing at my head!

Chapter Nine

The voice was familiar. Slowly, I looked up into an unsmiling face I'd seen once before. He was a big man, an inch or so over six feet, with an ordinary face and medium cut brown hair, dressed in a business suit.

The gun in his hand was familiar, too. He'd slugged me with it before.

I was annoyed and angry. "Now, what the hell do you want?" I demanded.

"Carol Rutledge," he said calmly, holding the gun a few inches from my head.

"Welcome to the club," I said. "But what makes you think I know anything about her?"

"I just guessed," he said. He nodded his head. "How about the girl?"

"She's not the one you're after."

He bent to peer in at her. "Very pretty, though. Carol has a birthmark. Perhaps I should check your girlfriend, just in case!"

"I've already checked," I said belligerently. "She doesn't have one."

"Maybe I'll look anyway. I might find something even more interesting."

"You so much as leer at her—" I began.

"And what?" he said, his grip tightening on the gun.

Slowly, I began inching my fingers toward the gun at my belt.

"By the way, it wouldn't be wise for you to get any closer to your gun—not unless you want your head blown off."

My fingers retreated, and in a sudden movement he reached in and snaked the weapon from the holster. He put it in his own pocket, then made a motion with his gun.

"All right, Miss Burke, get out."

"You're making a mistake," I said. "This isn't the girl you're after."

"I'm aware of that. But you seem to be making remarkable progress, and I'd like to give you an incentive. When you find out which girl it is, I'd like to be the first to know. To make sure I *am* the first, I'm taking the young lady with me. I'll give her back to you when you deliver Carol Rutledge to me."

"So you can kill her?"

"What we do with Carol is our concern, not yours. I'd suggest you find her real soon, because having a pretty girl like your friend around is going to be a temptation. And if you don't find Carol for us, we'll use your girlfriend here for entertainment purposes. We'll have a little get-together, perhaps about fifty males, and we'll take turns with her, one after the other, and when we're through you won't recognize her. Did you ever see a girl who's been raped by fifty men?"

"You bastard," I said: "You dirty bastard!"

He laughed.

"Chris!" Naomi said.

But I was expecting it this time. The gun in his fist shot out like a lightning bolt. I ducked, reached out with one hand to twist the ignition key. With the other hand I opened the door of the Porsche and pushed it hard into his stomach. He dropped the gun and staggered back. His grunt was lost in the roar of the engine blasting into life.

"Hang on!" I said.

I slammed the door shut, threw the car in gear, and pressed my foot into the accelerator. The car leaped ahead, spinning gravel. I pulled at the wheel, and the car responded and we pulled back onto the road. I glanced in the rearview mirror and saw him struggling to his feet. Then we turned a corner and were out of sight.

I breathed a sigh of relief, but I didn't slow the Porsche until we were in sight of the house. I guided us to a parking spot in the driveway and cut the motor. Silence returned.

Naomi entered my arms, and I held her close. She was trembling.

"Chris," she said, "I'm scared."

"It's all right," I told her. "It's all over."

"But suppose he comes back. Did you see the way he looked at me? He meant that about kidnapping me, about letting all those men—"

"Don't even think about it. The only reason he wanted you was because of Carol Rutledge."

"But he'll try again."

"Perhaps. But I hope to have found the girl before then. Once she's safe you'll be safe."

She forced a wan smile. "You're right. I'm behaving like an idiot. But, Chris, please find her as soon as you can and get this nightmare over with."

"I will," I promised. "But now let's go in and get some sleep. It looks like I've got a busy schedule tomorrow."

I helped her out of the car. Her hand was cold in mine, and I put a reassuring arm around her as we walked up the steps. There was no denying it had been a close call, and our safety depended on a number of things. If the car hadn't responded, if the door hadn't opened smoothly, if that blow had connected with my face—Naomi might at that very instant be suffering abuse instead of being close to me, our bodies touching.

We walked up the steps, and I fitted my key into the lock, and noiselessly pushed the door inward and

105

then closed it behind us. The house was dark and still, with only the shuffle of our footsteps as we walked softly across the large room.

At the foot of the stairs, she turned to me and I put my arms around her. Our bodies flowed together in a fervent embrace.

"Goodnight," I said.

She opened her mouth as though to say something else, then changed her mind and whispered, "Good-night, Chris."

I watched her go up the stairs, and then I went into the corridor leading to my own room. In the bedroom, I undressed in the dark, put on my pajamas, and climbed into bed. I should have been sleepy, but I wasn't. Too many things had happened in too short a time, and they were crowding my mind with thoughts.

I made an effort to force the unpleasant ones into my subconsciousness and consider the pleasant ones—like redheaded Naomi Burke, for example. I'd grown very fond of her in a very short time, and I didn't want anything bad to happen to her. It was ironic that in order to have her, I would have to be intimate with four other girls. Private detecting makes strange bed-fellows.

I was beginning to feel more relaxed, even drowsy, when I heard a noise. Instantly, I became alert. The sound came again. Footsteps on the stairway, caus-tiously descending.

Quickly, silently, I swept away the covers and swung from the bed. There was no time to dress; already whoever it was had reached the foot of the stairs. In seconds she could cross the large room and go out the front door.

I made my way across the dark bedroom, opened the door to the corridor and slipped out. I hurried down to the end of it and opened that door ever so slightly to look through. The person was not going out the front way; she was heading toward the rear of the house, and—

I blinked my eyes and hastily drew the door closed as she passed within a few feet of me. Then I opened the door wider to get a better look at the retreating figure. The light was dim, but the fact was unmistakable.

It was like something out of a bachelor's dream: Christina Ekberg, the tall lovely Swede, with a bath-towel in one hand and a bathing cap in the other, was going for a swim—nude!

Chapter Ten

I'd heard that in the Scandinavian countries the people liked to go in for nude swimming—even in the icy waters of that area. Apparently, Christina was homesick for the custom. The pool was heated to the mild temperature required for an afternoon swim, but this was three in the morning and the air was cold.

So was I, thinking of it. But the sight of the girl had given me other thoughts, too. She was a large girl built like a brick Amazon. Her huge breasts jutted out in front of her like ripe melons swaying in unison as she walked with a purposeful stride toward the rear of the house. Fascinated by the sight, I watched her naked buttocks twitch down the length of the room and then disappear.

With her long platinum hair trailing behind her, she had been like a lovely naked ghost haunting the house during the early morning hours. But she wasn't a ghost, I was sure of that. She was very real, and fantastically three-dimensional. I wondered if she had that diamond-shaped birthmark on her body.

There was only one way to find out. I hurried along the same path she had taken, across the room, through the alcove. I paused at the door exiting to the patio and pushed it open slightly. A blast of cold air met me and I hesitated, shivering. Then I thought of Christina out there without any clothes on at all and of what I had to do, and I opened the door and slipped out.

She was standing at one edge of the pool, stuffing her platinum hair under the bathing cap on her head. The towel lay in a heap at her feet where she had dropped it. She didn't look back to see me, and I stood there for a moment watching her.

She finished buckling her bathing cap and took a deep breath which swelled her taut-skinned breasts to even greater proportions. Then she stood for a moment like a piece of sculpture and slowly ran her hands down over her thighs, up over the arching curve of her hip, across the flat stomach and up to her pendulous breasts.

Then quietly, expertly, she slipped into the water.

The gentle splash awakened me from my trance, and I walked over to the pool and stood by the edge. As I watched, she swam slowly out to the center of the pool, her white body clearly visible in the underwater lights.

I squatted beside the towel, and watched and waited. It was a pleasure to watch her in motion. She was obviously enjoying herself, and she was very graceful while she was doing it. She paddled around and then swam underwater to the bottom where she did a few slow-motion dance steps. She surfaced and came swimming back and didn't see me until she was holding onto the edge.

She said "Oh!" in surprise, but she was obviously not embarassed by her nakedness.

"Mr. Sly, what are you doing up at this hour?"

"I was going to ask you the same question?"

"I'm swimming."

"I suspected that. But why?"

"Because I like to, of course. I used to do it all the time when I was back home."

"In the nude?"

"Of course. It's much more fun that way. I wear a bikini here because I have to, not because I want to. Come on in."

I had a feeling it would be much more fun in the nude. The water magnified her already immense proportions to a point that was unbelievable. Besides, I had a job to do, and now was a remarkably opportune time to handle it. Before I could talk myself out of it, I stripped off my pajamas and slid into the water beside her.

I almost gasped with the shock. "It's like an iceberg!" I complained.

She laughed. "You'll get used to it. But you should go all the way."

Without warning, she pushed my head under. I came back up spluttering, with a desire for revenge. I reached for her, but laughing she swam away, her white legs churning the water, her face daring me to catch her. I went after her.

She swam the length of the pool with me right behind her, then turned, saw me coming, and pushed herself down toward the bottom. I reached the opposite side, tensed my legs, and jackknifed them to follow her through the silent waters. She skimmed along the concrete, and I went down on her like a Kamikaze and caught her in my arms.

She squirmed about to face me and I tightened the grip of my arms around her so she couldn't get away, and slowly we drifted back toward the surface of the pool.

There was no sound, and it seemed like we were the only two people in a private world of our own. The chase had been playful, but the capture was rapidly becoming more serious. The water had lost its coldness and seemed pleasantly warm. Or maybe it was because Christina's magnificent female body was molded tightly against me to keep me warm, her breasts mashed against my chest, our hips pressed together, our arms and legs entwined.

We surfaced, and without a word, but anxiously, hurriedly, we climbed onto the coping. She lay back, and I joined her. She opened her mouth to say something, but I placed my own mouth over hers, filled with a more important message, and we clung together, our actions and thoughts rapidly converging into the same plane.

For a long moment neither of us moved, and the world seemed to hang in silent stasis, and then slowly, deliberately my hands moved along her, and her breathing increased and she began to move her body. The tempo increased, like a stream rushing toward a waterfall, faster and faster, naked bodies tossing on whitecaps of pleasure. Her teeth nipped at my shoulder, and she let out a deep animal moan. I held her tightly to me as we rushed accelerating toward the waterfall, reached its edge—I felt my muscles contract, and the girl let out her breath in a slow, soft sigh—and we relaxed and rolled over the edge of the coping into the pool!

The water closed over us, shutting out the subtle night sounds. The light shimmered around us as we descended slowly, locked in the sensual satisfaction of the aftermath. Our feet briefly touched the concrete bottom of the pool, and then tension gone, fires quenched, we drifted lazily to the surface again.

I climbed out and then grabbed her hand and helped her out. She sat down at the edge. I sat down beside her, exhausted but happy.

She looked at me admiringly. "You are an excellent swimmer," she said.

"Thanks," I said, grinning at her. "You know a couple of good strokes yourself."

"Back home I used to do this regularly, but here I have to do it in secret so Miss Rice doesn't know. She would be very angry with us if she knew."

"I'm not planning to tell her," I said.

Droplets of water were standing out on our bodies, and goosepimples were starting to form. The air seemed suddenly cold. I grabbed the towel.

"We'd better dry off," I said.

She closed her eyes and leaned back, murmuring an affirmative answer. I hesitated briefly, awed by the sight of all that woman, and then began working in earnest, toweling her briskly, starting with the neck and shoulders, working down around the responding breasts, across the stomach and along the legs. She purred softly with an animal contentment as I rubbed her all over until her skin glowed and I was satisfied that she was not Carol Rutledge.

"That was stimulating," she cooed when I finished.

"It certainly was," I agreed.

She laughed, seeing the truth of my statement. Then she took the towel from my hands and rubbed it over my body until I knew that I wasn't Carol Rutledge either.

"Do you do this often?" I asked her. "Swimming at night, I mean."

"One a week, maybe. I don't think Miss Rice

would approve, so I sneak out here when everyone is sleeping."

"She's probably never been in a bathing suit in her life," I said.

"She never does go in swimming," Christina admitted.

I could see why, with all the pulchritude she'd have as competition. "How about the other girls? Carmen, for example, or Mary Ellen, or Joanne?"

If she wondered why I happened to pick those three, her face didn't show it. She shook her platinum tresses.

"No," she said. "Janet wanted to swim nude with me, and I let her—once. Swimming wasn't what she had in mind, though."

"I've got a confession to make," I said. "It wasn't really what I had in mind, either."

She laughed. "I did enjoy our—er—swim together, though. I hope we can do it again."

"I hope so, too, Christina," I said sincerely.

I wasn't much of an outdoorsman, but I did want to brush up on my breast stroke.

"We'd better go in," she suggested. "I wouldn't want anyone to see us out here. If Miss Rice found out—"

I'd lose a job, I thought, just when I was getting close to finding the girl I had to find. I put on my pajamas, and Christina and I quietly returned to the house. We parted company at the foot of the stairs, where she leaned into me and gave me a kiss full on the lips. Then she whispered a "goodnight" and stealthily made her way up the stairs.

For a moment I stood watching her ascend. The shifting of those huge though well-proportioned buttocks was a marvelously graceful sight. Then I returned to my room and climbed into bed.

I was beginning to feel very tired, and sleep drifted over me. But I was making progress, that was certain. I'd narrowed the field of seven suspects to the three remaining girls: Carmen Cervantes, Mary Ellen Cuthbert, and Joanne Murray. One of these girls must have the elusive birthmark, and I'd have to find it.

It would bear looking into.

Chapter Eleven

I didn't bother setting an alarm, and the next morning I overslept. I permitted the luxury, since I'd put in a pretty full day's work the day before—if you can call checking birthmarks work. I opened my eyes, stretched, and stared at the ceiling. I switched on the light and looked at the clock: eleven-thirty.

I'd apparently been too exhausted to dream, which was a good thing. I had to conserve my energies for the last lap in my race against time, the Mafia, and Carol Rutledge. I was pleased that I was so close to my goal. Once this thing was settled, I could get down in earnest to courting Naomi the way a girl should be courted.

A knock came at the door, interrupting my thoughts.

"Come in," I said.

The door opened, and Annette cautiously poked her head in. "Monsieur is decent?" she asked.

I had to grin at that, considering what had happened between us the previous night. Possibly she was shy when the lights were on. In the dark, however, she was bold, even inventive. But I remembered she didn't want anyone to know, so I played it straight.

"Yes, Annette," I told her. "Monsieur is decent."

Satisfied, she came into the room but left the door open. "I was wondering if Monsieur would like to attend lunch with the ladies?"

I hadn't noticed it before, but my stomach seemed unusually empty. "Yes, I would."

I tossed aside the covers, got up and went to close the door. Annette looked at me, wonderingly.

About last night, Annette—" I began.

"Last night, Monsieur?"

"It's okay, no one can hear us. I just wanted to assure you that no one will know about it."

She cocked her head at me, he pretty features screwed into a quizzical look. "Know about what, Monsieur."

"Okay, if you want to play it safe," I said. "I just wanted you to know I wouldn't tell anyone about us."

She hesitated. "Monsieur has been drinking, perhaps?" she suggested.

"Of course not!" I said, getting a little annoyed with her insistence. "I'm sorry for snapping at you. Annette. Forgive me. But you were so wonderful last night—"

I reached to touch her, and she shrank away. "Oh, monsieur!" she said.

I paused, puzzled without knowing why. It was the same line she'd used the previous night, except it was different—different in more ways than the mood of the expression.

"Say that again," I told her.

She stared at me, uncomprehending.

"You said you wanted to be an actress. Let's see you say 'Oh, monsieur' as though you're in my arms and we're making love."

She hesitated briefly, then half-lidded her eyes, pursed her lips and said, "Oh, monsieur!"

"Annette, be frank with me. Were you in my room with me last night? Did we make love?"

She shook her head. "But no, monsieur. I have a fiance in Paris, a very terribly jealous man. If he thought I even looked at another man, he would go into a rage."

"I see," I said slowly. "Do me a favor and don't mention it to anyone, will you?"

She nodded, went to the door. "Will monsieur go down for lunch?"

"Yes," I said, absent-mindedly.

She went out and closed the door behind her. I sat down on the edge of the bed and considered this new development. Annette had no reason to lie to me, even if she were ashamed of what she'd done and regretted the action. Someone had come into my room the previous night, pretending to be Annette. I fell for the

French accent, especially with the distraction of her being so close. And of course, she didn't want the lights turned on—because then I could see it was not Annette.

But then the problem was, who was it? The answer seemed more obvious than I liked to think. The imposter had probably been Carol Rutledge. I'd held her in my arms and made love to her and never thought of looking for a birthmark or turning on the lights to see who it really was.

She'd said she would see me again, though. Possibly for a return match, in which she could pump me for information — or perhaps even to kill me, if she thought that might be necessary. If I hadn't mentioned it to Annette, I'd be defenseless against Carol; you don't ordinarily expect death at the hands of your love-partner.

I put on a bathrobe and went down the corridor to the bathroom, where I shaved, when the door opened and Miss Charlotte Rice came in. She saw me and stopped, her eyes widening. It was probably her first sight of a man without any clothing on. I was too startled to pick up the towel, and by that time the action would have been anti-climatical.

She uttered an "oh!" and turned, slamming the door behind her. Her feet made rapid sounds up the corridor.

I imagined I would get a lecture on door-locking,

but the prospect failed to bother me. I finished toweling myself dry, put on the bathrobe and went back to my room to dress.

A few minutes later, I arrived at the dining room to find all the girls there. I glanced briefly at Miss Rice, who turned away from my gaze and actually seemed to blush at some memory.

Janet Hooper didn't give me a second look, but that didn't matter; the only thing we had in common was that we both liked girls. Eva Slater's smile was not too welcoming either, and I decided that maybe she thought I wasn't her type. The others, including Naomi's, were honest and warm and friendly; Christina's glistening smile also imparted a secret knowledge, an empathy between us, that no one else knew.

We ate and made idle conversation and all the time I wondered which one of the girls had visited me in the dark pretending to be Annette. I tried to recall details of the girl's features and body and hair—and failed. I had thought it was Annette, so I remembered her as Annette. But it was not, I was sure of it.

Assuming it had been Carol Rutledge, it must be one of the three girls I hadn't yet checked for the birthmark; Carmen Cervantes with the long black hair and the dark flashing eyes; Mary Ellen Cuthbert, the southern girl with the accent you could cut with a mint julep; Joanne Murray, the baby-faced creature who was trying to convince herself she was another

Marilyn Monroe.

None of them seemed the type, but I remembered that Carol Rutledge was a capable actress; she'd proved that with her impersonation of Annette in my bedroom. She could also adopt another phoney accent, or an artificial attitude, in addition to changing her appearances.

After lunch, Joanne Murray bounced up to me and wanted to know how about a game of ping-pong? I recalled what had happened at the last game we'd played, when her halter had fallen off under the stress and strain, and it was an inviting prospect. However, I had more pressing problems, so I told her maybe later, gave Naomi a reassuring nod and started for the library.

"Mr. Sly," a cold voice said behind me, and I paused while Charlotte Rice came up to me, her face grim. "May I suggest that hereafter when you're in the bathroom that you lock the door?"

"You certainly may, Miss Rice," I said. And since I was annoyed by her prudish attitude, I added: "And may I suggest that the human body, while not a thing of beauty in every case, is certainly nothing to be ashamed of. If you put on a bikini and joined the other girls by the pool, perhaps your mind would be a lot healthier too."

With that, I turned and walked away, leaving her to splutter indignantly. I closed the library doors behind me, and I realized that I'd made a mistake. This was not time to get the woman sore at me, not when I was so close to my goal. Now she would watch me like a hawk-eyed chaperone, perhaps even try to make trouble when I already had trouble enough. It was another incentive to get the job over with as soon as possible.

I sat on the edge of the desk, picked up the phone and dialed a number. I got Devlin's secretary on the phone and said, "This is Christopher Sly. I'd like to speak to your husband, please."

There was an uncertain pause and she said, "My what?"

"Isn't Oscar your husband?" I said.

"Not any more. I was his fifth wife, and sometimes he forgets we're not married any more."

"I see. By the way, I meant to ask whose Jaguar XKE that was parked out front when I was there. It's a beautiful body, and built for speed."

"It's mine," she said. "The car and I are alike in those respects—in case you're interested."

"I'm interested," I said automatically, and then I thought of Naomi and felt like a heel. I said, "But right now, I'd like to talk to Oscar, if I may."

"Just a second."

The line went silent for an instant, and then Oscar Devlin said, "How're things going, Sly?"

"Not bad."

"Keeping up the pace?"

"Yes," I told him. "I've got to get in touch with Dave. It's very important."

"Dave had to fly to New York, but he should be back tonight. Any message I can give him?"

"No. Just tell him to call me as soon as he gets in."

"Will do. Oh, Sly?"

"Yeah?"

"Keep it up."

"Keep what up?."

"The good work," he chuckled.

"Yeah," I said.

We hung up. One thing I wanted of Dave was protection for Naomi. The hood probably wasn't too happy that I'd given him a sore stomach, and he might come back looking for revenge. I didn't want anything to happen to Naomi because of me.

There was a sound behind me, and I turned to find Carmen Cervantes standing in the doorway. She was wearing a white low-cut blouse that showed the crevice between her breasts, a many-colored skirt that flared from her hips, and a pair of sandals. Her long black hair was pulled tightly along the side of her head and fastened in back, from which point it cascaded in an ebony stream down her back. A blood-red rose was bobby-pinned behind her left ear. She gave me a smile, and her dark eyes flashed.

"Hello," I said. It was an inadequate beginning, but

all I could think of at the time.

She nodded acknowledgement and said, "Could I speak with you for a few minutes, Mr. Sly?"

"Of course, Carmen. Come in."

She came in, her skirt whirling, and closed the door. She hesitated, looked at the door, made a rapid decision, and locked it. I wondered what that was all about, but I didn't ask. I had the impression she was going to tell me. The thought went through my mind that she was Carol Rutledge and she was about to whip a derringer from her underclothing and shoot me, but I dismissed that thought because it was too unpleasant. More pleasant were the recollections of the hungry looks Carmen had given me on several occasions.

She put her hands on her hips and sauntered toward me. She stopped in front of me so that I had a view of her neckline and the deep vee starting above the material.

"Do you think I am pretty?" she asked.

"Yes," I said.

This pleased her. She stepped back and cupped her breasts in her hands.

"And do you think I have nice breasts?"

"Yes," I said "At least, what I can see of them."

"I will show you more," she announced.

She took hold of the blouse and pulled it up over head, worked free of it and tossed it into a nearby chair. Her breasts were full and large, restrained by a black bra that showed an immense amount of cleavage. She reached in back of her for the fastening hooks, unsnapped them, and slipped the bra and straps from her breasts and shoulders.

The breasts did not fall. They stood out firmly, bronzed and beautiful.

"Do you like them?" she wanted to know.

I nodded eagerly. "Very nice," I said, wondering what was going to happen next.

"They are real, too," she said proudly.

"I'll bet they are," I said.

"Here, feel them if you don't believe me."

She grabbed my hands and pressed them to her. I felt them.

"Yes," I said, hoarsely. "Yes, they're real all right." I wasn't complaining, but I did wonder what had inspired this performance.

"Some girls sag when they don't have support," she said, "but not me. Even—" she hesitated, looked around the room, then whispered confidently, "even Christina, the Swedish girl, has this problem."

"Really," I said.

She nodded, then stepped back, "Legs?" she said. "How are these for legs?"

She took the hem of her many-colored skirt and lifted it up high above her hips and the black panties she wore. Her legs were long and smooth and perfect.

I nodded. "Very nice," I managed.

"Here," she said, coming toward me, "feel how smooth the skin is."

I felt how smooth the skin was and admitted it. The room was suddenly getting very hot, and I held my breath as she stepped back again and pushed the skirt down over her hips and stepped out of it Then she walked around the room in her panties and slippers, her hands on her hips, her firm breasts jiggling, her perfect legs moving in almost a dance step. Then she stopped in front of me expectantly.

"What do you think?" she wanted to know.

I stared at that long hair, the deep eyes, the bare throat and shoulders and breasts, the hips covered with thin panties, the smooth tapering legs. I could feel my breathing becoming heavier, my heart moving at a greater speed.

"I think you're a very sexy girl, Carmen," I said honestly.

"Good," Carmen said eagerly. "Then, what are we waiting for?"

She hooked her thumbs into the elastic tops of her panties, pushed them down over hips and thighs and stepped out of them. Then, with an animal cry, she threw herself at me.

The maneuver surprised me, and we went down on the library floor in a tangle of arms and legs. I was glad she'd locked the door because Carmen's assault was much too overwhelming to be denied — if I'd thought of denying it, which I didn't. The business with the breasts and the prancing around had gotten me in the mood from which there was only one escape.

Her hands and fingers were frantically moving about my clothing, unbuttoning buttons, unzipping zippers, tugging at the belt, pulling at the shirt. Her enthusiasm was contagious, and I found myself infected with it.

She pulled me to her and rolled over on the floor, her breasts flattening under me. I placed my hands on her hips and pulled her toward me until it was impossible to get any closer. Her dark eyes were slitted with passion, her face esctatic, as she shivered with delightful sensations permeating her. Her arms circled my neck, holding me in a tight embrace, her breathing became as ragged as my own, our hearts staccatoed in unison, matching our movements.

Her teeth found my shoulder, bit savagely into it, and then a torrent of frantic Spanish flowed from her lips, as we were lifted on a roaring tide of passion that crescendoed to the highest peak of sensual excitement, exploded in fleshly breakers, and then ebbed slowly into the calm of the aftermath...

For a while we lay together on the soft carpeting of the library floor. It was minutes after I heard the sound that I became aware that someone was pounding on the library door.

"Mr. Sly," Charlotte Rice's voice came through,

"are you in there?"

I motioned Carmen to be silent. "Yes," I said, "I'm busy right now."

"Is Carmen in there with you?" she asked.

"No, of course not," I told her.

Another female voice—Naomi's—came through the door. "I saw her upstairs just a few minutes ago."

Charlotte Rice grunted, but she moved away. Good old Naomi, I thought. I owed a lot to that girl.

I got up, helped Carmen to her feet. A light film of moisture was on her skin, making it glisten, and a few wisps of black hair made commas on her forehead.

"You'd better get your clothes on and leave before Rice comes back down."

She nodded, and began pulling on her clothes. "Do I get the part?"

I stared at her. "The what?"

"Don't be angry with her. Naomi told me why you are *really* here."

"She did?" I couldn't believe it.

Carmen pulled the black panties securely around her hips, started slipping her breasts into the bra. "She said you were a talent scout for a big producer, and I should be very nice to you and maybe you would give me a part in a picture." Her dark eyes flashed at me. "Did you like the way I was nice to you?"

"I certainly did, Carmen," I said, "and I was very much impressed with your talents. The very next time

I have a part that will fit you, I'll think of you."

I was also impressed even more with Naomi's talents. She was a clever girl. She'd wanted to help me, and she had. Carmen did't have the birthmark either.

"Hurry!" Naomi whispered through the door. "Rice is coming back down stairs'!'

I opened the door and Naomi thrust her head through.

"No, but that narrows it to two: Mary Ellen Cuthbert and Joanne Murray. If the next one has the birthmark we'll know she's the one I'm after; if she doesn't, we'll know it's the other girl. Either way, I can't lose."

Carmen hurried over to us, stuffing her blouse into her skirt. Naomi hustled her out, calling over her shoulder, "Lock the door."

I locked the door again, went to the phone and dialed a number. At the other end it rang twice, there was a click, and an unenthusiastic female voice said, "The ti-yem is two-twelve — and forty seconds." I glanced at my watch, which was two minutes slow, but I didn't bother to correct it. I was listening to the angry, determined stomp of Miss Charlotte Rice coming across the large room, and the pounding on the door that followed.

"Open the door," Miss Rice demanded. "I know you've got Carmen in there."

I placed the receiver on the desk and went to open the door. Charlotte Rice rushed in, her grey head swiveling suspiciously.

"I told you I was making a very important call. Now please don't bother me."

I returned to the phone, placed it to my ear. "The ti-yem is two-twelve—exactly," the voice said. Out of the corner of my eye I noticed the woman sniffing around the drapes and bending to look under the piano and the desk.

"All right," I said loudly into the phone, "call me back when you have the time."

I hung up and turned to face Charlotte Rice, who had given up the search.

"Now, what was it you wanted?" I asked innocently.

She smiled humorously, a showing of even teeth that was not intended to be friendly. "You're clever, Mr. Sly, but not clever enough." She was holding a blood-red rose idly in her hand, which I tried to ignore, "While you were supposed to be telephoning, I made a call of my own—to Majestic Studios, and more precisely, to Oscar Devlin's boss. He was very sympathetic. So sympathetic, in fact, that you are being replaced, effective when the new man arrives tomorrow morning!"

She turned toward the door, paused there. "I suggest you have your things packed so you'll be ready to leave without any delay."

I hardly ever have the desire to clobber a woman, but the thought occurred to me as Charlotte Rice swept triumphantly from the room. Defeated, I thought glumly, with victory so near.

The intercom buzzer sounded on the phone. I picked it up, punched the button.

"Monsieur, this is Annette. There is a long-distance call for you on line four."

"Thanks," I said into the phone.

"Chris, this is Dave," a familiar voice said.

I thought I detected an unfamiliar note of panic in the voice.

"Yes, Dave, where are you?. I've been trying to get in touch with you."

"I'm in New York. I've been doing some special checking. Have you found what you were looking for?"

"Not quite. One more will decide it."

"Good, but there's something else you've got to know, Chris, but I can't tell you over the phone. I'm going to jet back to LA tonight. I'll meet you at your apartment—the other one—at eight o'clock. Be there, Chris, because it's literally a matter of life or death."

It was the inevitable question. "Whose?" I asked him.

He hesitated only briefly. "Yours," he said.

Chapter Twelve

"I heard you were going to leave us," Joanne Murray said.

"That's what they tell me," I said.

I was in my room, ostensibly packing. Actually, there wasn't much to pack, just a few things I could throw together in a few minutes. Joanne sneaked in to talk to me, and we closed the door so no one could see here there. Even if Charlotte Rice discovered us together, it would make little difference as far as my job was concerned. And I wanted Joanne there, so I could complete the job I'd started out to do.

One of the girls was supposed to have a diamond-shaped birthmark in a place not normally seen by the world. So far I'd eliminated five out of the seven, and only two remained to investigate. Logically, it didn't matter which of the two I chose, but accessibility was a factor. Mary Ellen Cuthbert, while a sweet girl, was not overly friendly. Joanne Murray, while a sweet girl, *was* overly friendly, and if my plans worked out she would soon get even more overly friendly.

"I'm going to miss you, Chris," she said.

"Maybe the new man can play ping pong, too," I suggested.

She pouted. "That's not what I mean, and you know it."

I laughed. "I know. Come over here beside me," I said, patting the bed. "I want to talk to you."

She was wearing her short-shorts that appeared to be glued on, but I noticed there was a button and a zipper on the side, and a pair of snug panties underneath. She sat down beside me and crossed her slim youthful legs. Her midriff was bare, and she was wearing only the brief halter tied in back that had failed her during a crucial moment in a ping pong game. The halter was not doing the job now, but it was trying. The odds against it, however, were tremendous, and the cloth had slipped down almost to the tips of her creamy woman's flesh with the deep valley separating them. I recalled pleasantly how she had looked naked to the waist.

She inhaled deeply and gave her blonde head a toss. "Did I tell you that my agent said I might become another Marilyn Monroe?"

"I believe you mentioned it," I said, edging closer to her on the bed. " But I think you make a first-rate Joanne Murray."

"That's what I like most about you, Chris," she confided. "You think of me as a person, not merely as a sex symbol."

"You *are* a person, Joanne," I said. I gently touched her arm with my fingers, moved the fingers along the arm, barely touching it. "You're a distinct, individual human being, and you should act like yourself."

"Of course, there's nothing wrong with looking like Marilyn Monroe," she said.

"Not a thing in the world," I agreed.

She turned to face me, and I put out my other hand and took her shoulder in that and pulled her toward me. She smiled and didn't resist. My arms went around in back of her, my fingers touching the knot holding her halter in place, and she put her arms around my waist and turned her face expectantly upward, closing the eyes, parting the lips slightly. In that instant, my probing fingers destroyed the knot, and the halter fell between us.

"Chris," she said, and her eyes opened in surprise.

I didn't answer. I kissed her on the cheek and on the corner of the mouth and then full on the mouth, and she closed her eyes again. Our tongues worked into each others' mouths, and I ran my hands along her smooth naked back. She moaned without leaving my mouth and twisted her body slightly to allow my hands greater freedom.

She clung to me, her lips working fervently, her breath coming in short irregular gasps. The kiss seemed to be becoming more than a kiss to her; it was practically an entire act of love, a consummation all in itself.

My hand slid down along the slope of her side to the edge of the shorts, to the button and the zipper. She stiffened perceptibly, and took my hand in hers and returned it to its former position.

"You know," she said, "I thought you'd never make a pass at me. I was beginning to feel insulated."

She began nibbling at my ear and rubbing herself against me. My hand slipped from its resting place again and glided slowly downward, across her stomach this time, to the brief shorts. Her skin felt cold suddenly, as her hand went down to mine. Before it could touch me, I had flicked open the buttons and was tugging at the zipper.

"No, Chris, please," she said. "I don't want to."

That one stopped me cold. "You don't want to? What about all these preliminaries? The kissing, the bare bosom bit? What do you think all this is leading up to, a game of ping pong?"

"Don't be angry with me, Chris," she begged.

"Angry, who's angry? You just lead me on, get me all hot and bothered, and then you expect to nonchalantly slam the gate and expect me to just forget it!"

She hesitated. "You won't believe this," she said finally, "but—but, well, I'm a virgin. I'm twenty-two years old and a virgin."

"Don't you think it's about time for a change, then?" I suggested.

"I—I guess I've got what you might call a psychological block. I'm supposed to be a sexpot, someone who knows and has experienced everything about sex. And I try to act the part—at least above the navel. But I've never been able to go all the way. Never. I wanted to with you, honest I did, but when you started touching me I almost screamed. It was terrible." She looked away. "You probably hate me."

"No, I don't hate you, Joanne. I think I'm just beginning to understand you."

I reached for her, but she pulled away and stood up.

She snatched up the halter, hastily tied it in place. I didn't stop her.

"I—I'd better go," she said. "I'm sorry."

She turned, opened the door, and fled down the corridor. I didn't go after her. I was too busy wondering if she really did have a psychological block that made her keep her panties on—or was it that she had a birthmark she didn't want me to see?

Chapter Thirteen

I knew instinctively that Mary Ellen Cuthbert would not be an easy person to inspect for birthmarks in intimate places. In fact, she was going to be damned difficult. I'd met the type before. She was probably the daughter of some retired Kentucky Colonel, and she would be very shy and perhaps even operate on the theory of the old school—that as far as men were concerned ladies were solid from the knees up.

It wouldn't be easy, but it *did* have to be done. I might not be around tomorrow. Besides, I was seeing Dave Keller at eight, and I wanted to give him the name of the girl we were after.

Time was running out. I went upstairs, knocked at the door, and waited.

"Come in," she said in a thick southern accent.

I opened the door and went it. Mary Ellen looked up with interest and surprise, as evidenced by an eyebrow that climbed skyward at my entrance. She was lying on her stomach on the bed reading a book, wearing an organdy nightgown that was feminine, frilly,

137

and ruffled. She sat up and swung her legs from the bed. As she did so, the nightgown parted to show a glimpse of smooth curved leg, and she calmly rearranged the material to cover the exposed flesh.

"Mr. Sly," she said, smiling demurely, "this *is* a pleasant surprise. I thought you were much too busy with the other girls to notice little old me."

Carefully, firmly, I closed the door behind me. "Not at all," I said. "In fact, I was hoping you and I could have an intimate heart to heart talk."

"Just how intimate would you like our talk?" she asked.

Some southern accents leave me cold, but Mary Ellen's was rather warm and personal and I found myself enjoying the casualness of it. Also, there was the fact that under the frilly nightgown she obviously had a body to be proud of. I recalled seeing it displayed in the bikini when I'd first glimpsed the patio and its lovely female occupants. She didn't have as much as some of the other girls, but she had enough, and it was all of good quality.

I moved toward her, wondering how I should approach her. She seemed to sense my uncertainty, and she patted the bed beside her.

"Why don't you just sit right down here, Mr. Sly, and we'll have our talk."

I sat down on the bed beside her and she placed a casual hand on my leg, smiling as I jumped with the surprise of the contact.

"Now, then—" I began.

"I understand this is your last day with us," she said.

"I'm afraid so. It's unfortunate I couldn't have gotten to know you better."

"Yes, it is," she said, "but I'm sure we can make up for lost time. Would you like to help me undress, Mr. Sly?"

I stared at her. Her hand was physically on my leg; I wondered if she were verbally pulling it. However, her pretty features, framed by the soft brown hair, were quite serious.

"Yes, yes, of course," I said.

"Well?"

I reached out for her and she leaned toward me. I took the frilly nightgown in my fingers and slowly peeled it back from her creamy skin. It was tied in front, and I untied it. The nightgown fell away from her, and I lifted it from her body and let it drop on the bed.

"Gracious," she exclaimed, "that feels good—the touch of your hands, I mean. Will you kiss me, Mr. Sly?"

I kissed her. I took her china face in my hands and I kissed her.

"Kiss me again," she begged.

I kissed her again, on the shoulder this time.

"And here," she said.

139

I kissed her there.

"Kiss me all over," she insisted. "I want you to kiss me all over."

I kissed her all over.

"Do everything to me."

I did everything to her ...

Chapter Fourteen

It was a few minutes of eight as I parked the Porsche in its familiar stall at my apartment. The place woulld probably resemble a morgue until I got used to it. The plush and sensual atmosphere at the home of the 'seven deadly sinners' had managed to spoil me, and I'd miss it. I hadn't brought my things with me, because I was going to return to it with Dave, so he could make whatever arrangements were necessary to take care of Carol Rutledge.

That was my surprise to him, and I wondered what his was to me. Something about a matter of my life or my death, he'd said over the phone. It sounded quite serious.

I walked up the steps and across the courtyard, my heels making sharp sounds in the silence. My apartment was darkened, and Dave was not outside waiting. I applied my key to the lock and walked in, closing the door behind me. I reached for the light switch, flicked it on, and the room lights flared into brilliance.

"You're very prompt, Mr. Sly," a male voice said.

I stared at him. It was the hood who had clobbered me in my apartment and who had tried to kidnap Naomi the night before. He was sitting casually in a chair, legs crossed, smiling, his hair neatly combed, his business suit unwrinkled, looking very much like a business man—except for his usual exception, the gun in his hand.

"What do you want now?" I asked him.

"You really shouldn't be too impatient, Mr. Sly Because when we're through talking here, I'm going to kill you."

He said it calmly enough, with a sincere smile, but the tone of it made me feel cold.

I backed into a chair and stared at him. He'd taken my .38 special from me the night I was in the Porsche, and my spare was in the headboard of the bedroom a long way from where we were.

"Why?" I asked.

He shrugged. "A number of reasons. The one I'm really interested in, however, is revenge."

"Revenge?"

"Yes, nothing more complicated than that. You slammed a car door into my groin last night—"

"It was in self-defense," I said.

"It hurt," he said. "It might even have injured me permanently. Fortunately, it didn't. But it could have. And I don't like pain, Mr. Sly, not when I'm on the receiving end. So I'm going to kill you."

One think I had to do was stall for time. Perhaps, when Dave Keller got here, the distraction would enable me to get out of this mess. A matter of life and death, Dave had said. It was ironic that it had turned out like that so soon after the prediction.

Except perhaps it was not so ironic after all. Perhaps —the thought catapulted through my mind—Dave Keller had known about it all along!

Suppose Dave himself were working for the Mafia. He could easily have set me up for the trap I'd walked into.

"You're very quiet," the man said, amused. "Are you saying your prayers?"

I ignored the sarcasm. "You said there were other reasons for killing me. Like what, for example?"

"For example, I don't like you," he said. "I do like your girl friend Naomi, though; she's very nice. After you're gone, I expect to visit her and see that she doesn't get lonely."

"You bastard!"

"Mainly, though, there are business reasons. You were brought into the picture for a particular purpose—"

"To find Carol Rutledge," I supplied.

"Exactly. You accomplished the job in record time, and we're quite proud of your resourcefulness. However, you also worked yourself out of a job."

"So why can't we just leave it at that?"

He shook his head. "Because you know too much. You may not realize it, but you do. We have no choice but to get rid of you. Not that I mind, of course. In fact, I'll enjoy watching you die."

I believed he would. Casually, I glanced around the room looking for a weapon. I didn't want to go, but if I had to, I'd put up a struggle. I just hoped I could get in one good Karate blow before he put a hole in me.

"How does Dave Keller fit into the picture?"

"Exactly the way he told you. If you're expecting him to show up and rescue you, you may as well forget it. I took care of him, just before you arrived. I was waiting for him, just as I was for you. I didn't want to get blood on your carpet, so I dumped him in on your bed."

He sighed impatiently and thumbed back the hammer of his weapon.

"This conversation is beginning to bore me," he said. "Do you have any final words?"

"A few. I'd like to know how you found out I was going to meet Dave here tonight. And how you know who Carol Rutledge is when I didn't tell you."

He grinned at the secret. "Sure, I'll tell you, Sly. You'll probably be very much amused. In fact, I have the suspicion you'll die laughing."

He frowned at a sound.

"Yes?" I prompted.

He waved his head in an irritated gesture for me to

be quiet, and I tensed myself in the chair. The bedroom door crashed open, and instinctively he brought his gun to bear on the figure standing there. At that moment, I sprang from the chair and slammed the edge of my hand into his wrist.

He yelled, and the gun clattered onto the floor and skidded across the carpet, coming to rest against the wall. My impetus landed me heavily on top of him, and the chair toppled over and we both went down on the floor in a scramble of arms and legs.

We rolled, panting, seeking leverage, and he came out on top. He was not nearly so calm now, but there was a determined look on his features. He raised a fist, brought it down savagely toward my face. I moved my head, fast, and the blow landed heavily on the floor. He winced with the sudden pain and shifted balance slightly and I kept him going with a blow to the neck that lifted him almost to his feet. I slammed a fist into his abdomen and rolled him off me.

I scrambled to my feet and whirled to face him. But his outstretched hand had closed about the weapon on the floor and he brought it up with a triumphant grin on his face. His finger tightened on the trigger.

There was a sudden roar, and the side of his face exploded. The impact whirled him over on his stomach, where he lay quiet and unmoving.

I looked up. "Thanks."

"Don't mention it," Dave Keller said.

My spare .38 was hanging limply in his hand, and he was walking toward me supporting himself with one hand against the wall. His clothes were wrinkled and bloody and there was a hole in his shirt from a bullet. I went to help him, but before I got there he fell in a heap on the floor.

I rushed to the phone and called an ambulance. Then I called the police station and got Lieutenant Prine on the phone. Even while I was telling him the story I could hear the ambulance sirens shrieking toward us.

"This is going to be a full night for you, Sly," he said. "We've got a lot of questions to ask you."

"How do you mean?"

"We got a call about a half hour ago from Charlotte Rice, Somebody apparently broke into the place, ripped the clothes off one of the girls and tried to kill her."

I felt cold. "Which girl?" I asked him.

"Joanne Murray," he said. "Know her?"

"I know her," I said.

"But not nearly as well as you wanted to," he said.

I forced myself to be patient. "What are you driving at, Prine?"

"One of the girls overheard a conversation between you and the Murray girl in your bedroom. She wouldn't let you do what you wanted. It's easy to see what might have happened. You were angry, so you went up to see her and tried to force your attentions on the girl. She resisted, so you hit her and tore the clothes from her."

"That's not true!" I said, more hotly than I'd intended. "Why don't you ask her?"

"Because she's in the hospital with head injuries," he said, "and is unconscious. Meanwhile, we'd like to have you drop down to the station tomorrow morning, and we'll have a little chat about it."

"I'll be there," I said.

"Fine—and don't leave on any sudden trips to Mexico."

I answered him by slamming the receiver down on the hook. I wasn't worried about any charges he might attempt, but his attitude annoyed me.

The ambulance arrived and rushed Dave to the hospital. The other body they didn't have to hurry with; he was dead. The police arrived and took pictures and asked questions. Finally, around midnight, they left, taking with them the body and also my .38 special Dave had used.

The body I could get along without, but the weapon I could have a use for, at least for moral support. I knew my job wasn't over yet. I had one more trip to make, with many questions I'd have to have answered myself, and with luck I'd get the answers to those questions and maybe even come back alive!

Chapter Fifteen

It was close to one in the morning as I guided the Porsche up the winding road into the Hollywood Hills. I pulled the car into the curved driveway and parked in front of the silent white mansion overlooking the city.

I got out, walked up the steps, applied my key to the lock, and went in. It was dark, but I didn't switch on a light. I walked through the dimness as quietly as I could, crossed the large center room, and went into the corridor leading to the room I'd occupied.

I pushed open the door, switched on the light, closed the door behind me. Naomi was sitting on the bed, my .38 special—the one the hood had taken from me when she and I were parked down the road—in her hand. She looked up.

"I knew you'd come back," she said unemotionally.

There was no welcome in her voice. It was matter-of-fact, almost toneless, yet a little weary.

"Would you like to tell me about it?" I said.

"I think you're the one who's got to do some explaining," she said. "You lied to me. Joanne Murray is not Carol Rutledge."

I stared at her. "What?"

Her face became a mask of anger. "Don't give me the innocent routine. I don't know how long you knew I was hired by the Mafia, but it's obvious you did know. Otherwise, why lie to me about which girl it is. It was a great plan. As soon as you pointed her out, I was to step in and kill her."

"As you killed Frank Sheldon?" I suggested.

She grinned. "Eliot did that. He's my husband, the one who visited you in your apartment, and also who saw us parking. He tried to control himself, but he gets jealous sometimes." Her face grew angry again. "If you'd hurt him with that door routine—"

I didn't tell her he was dead. "How do you know Joanne is not Carol Rutledge?"

"After you left, I went up to her room. I got in without her seeing me, and I hit her with your gun. I was going to shoot her and then leave the weapon behind to involve you. And then I thought I'd better check. So I ripped her clothes off—and there was no birthmark."

I was silent. I looked at her, wondering if this was really the girl I'd almost fallen in love with.

She motioned with the gun. "I'm not fooling around, Chris. I've got a job to do, and I've got to do it or else I'll get in trouble myself. Which girl is it?"

"I don't know," I said.

"I don't want to have to kill you," she said.

"I'm telling you the truth," I said. "None of the girls has a diamond-shaped birthmark."

She searched my face. The gun wavered, indecisively. "You're lying."

The bedroom door swung open noiselessly. "He's not lying," Charlotte Rice said calmly.

Startled, Naomi swung the gun toward the intruder. I stepped toward her and knocked the weapon clattering from her hand.

"My turn," Charlotte said.

She took a determined stride and swung a fist that connected with Naomi's chin. The redhead staggered back and slumped to the floor, unconscious.

"Not a bad right for an old lady," Charlotte Rice said proudly.

"I don't get it," I said to her. "How do you fit into the picture?"

"Right in the center," she said. "Here, I'll show you."

She smiled. It was a strangely pleasant smile. And she took off her glases, and removed two pins from her hair to let it fall gracefully down around her shoulders.

"I'll have to wash the grey out later," she said.

She unbuttoned the front of her dress and stepped out of it clad only in panties and bra, and with a series of quick, uninhibited motions she stripped herself of

150

those undergarments. She stood naked in the center of the room, stretching and running her hands along her hips and breasts.

"You're magnificent!" I gasped.

"Thanks," she said. "You weren't so bad yourself."

I wondered what she meant by that, and then I thought of a rendezvous that had been consummated completely in the dark.

"Annette?" I said.

"Oui, Monsieur," she said.

"But what about Carol Rutledge?"

She walked across the room, brushing tantalizingly against me. "It's been a long time since I've had a man," she said. "We'll talk about Carol Rutledge later, when we have more time."

She stretched out on my bed and held out her arms invitingly toward me. I joined her, and during the next ten minutes I found out about Carol Rutledge and about the birthmark, which had in a sense been under my nose all this time.

THE END

151